I0602397

LINDA SEALY KNOWLES

# Abby's New Life

## By Linda Sealy Knowles

ISBN-13: 978-1-0882-4980-2

To my brother, Michael Sealy.
Thank you for your love and support
Of my writing career.

G old, Gold!" Exciting words rang out in the streets of San Francisco causing men and women to push and shove their way through the crowd to see the next lucky prospector.

Earlier in May, ten-year-old Mason Waters had heard another prospector yelling about his find, which made him laugh. "There's another lucky old fool who will get his gold dust and spend it all in the saloons before nightfall."

Jackson Waters, who ran a sawmill operation at the edge of town, laughed with his nephew as he took a break. He bent down to wash his face in the cool water. "I agree with you, son, but those old fellows won't remember how hard they worked to get that little gold dust. They are ready to kick their heels over their heads and have some fun with a pretty gal."

Jackson dipped his shallow pan into the water, then lowered himself to his knees to wash his neck. Something shiny glittered from the bottom of his pan, and he knew in a moment what he saw—gold dust.

Trying hard to stay calm as they worked, both uncle and nephew dammed up a small area. They grabbed their wooden sluice and shoveled buckets of dirt and sand, then they ran a stream of water over the sluice as they gently shook the wooden box from side to side. As the soil dissolved away, the golden sand and nuggets sank to the bottom. The hardworking uncle and nephew had just went from being dirt poor to rich in a twinkle of an eye.

---

## Chapter 1

---

San Francisco
1865

Oh, Mama, I just don't know what I'll do without you, Abby Mills thought as she pressed her tired forehead on the glass window. The street below was busy. Abby shook her head as she thought about the hundreds of people who still came to the small town of San Francisco to try their hand at finding gold.

Loosening the top button on her shirt waist, she closed the window in her mama's room, but the tromping footsteps still resounded through the closed window. Abby smiled to herself at the sound below of a miner's gleeful announcement at the top of his lungs. "Gold, I found gold!"

When she peered down, the miner's horse reared as the man slapped its leg, then headed toward the land office to stake his claim.

Abby pulled down the raggedy brown-paper shade and closed the soft green curtains. The air in the room had a musty odor, but it was still warm. Fanning herself with an oriental fan, she inched toward the bed and sat next to her mama's frail body. Abby pushed the loose hairs away from her mama's once soft, creamy complexion. Her skin was so white that the pale blue veins in her eyelids were visible. Abby watched her mama sleep and thought of better days.

As a small child, she remembered how beautiful her mama used to be. Isabella Mills had golden hair and twinkling green eyes, mesmerizing any man who looked her way. While she was working as the madam of the Red Dog Saloon, the place had an excellent reputation for serving quality liquor and clean entertainment. She worked long hours each night, entertaining customers by singing and serving the card tables in the back room. Mama was protective of the few girls who worked on the second floor. Sal, a tall, muscular Black man, stood at the base of the staircase to make sure the men didn't overstay their visit and that they behaved themselves while being entertained by the ladies.

As she gazed at her mother's hands, memories of her childhood floated back. Memories of sitting in the kitchen counting the hours until she could have dinner with her mama. "Is it six o'clock yet?"

Lucinda, the head housekeeper, scolded, "If you ask me that one more time, I'm going to make you peel the onions that make my eyes and nose run." The big-busted housekeeper always wore her red hair in a messy bun and looked quite stern as she slapped the big carving knife on the counter. "You know your mama sleeps all day and you haven't been home from school very long. Besides, I'm tired from walking all the way to that schoolhouse to retrieve you."

Abby remembered being lonely, even when she went to school, because the other children were not allowed to play with her due to her mother's occupation. Once when the teacher witnessed the way the children shunned her, she called her over to her desk.

"Abby, I have some new books that I thought you might like to read while sitting under the shade tree. You may take a book or two home, but be sure to bring them back. Once you have read them, you can take another one." Miss Gertrude never spoke to her about her living conditions, but she must have discerned that Abby was a good child and had the desire to learn.

After school Abby wasn't allowed to go outside, so she had to stay in the kitchen until her mama came down to dinner. The big saloon and parts of the upstairs were off limits.

"May I cook the dumplings today," Abby asked Lucinda. "I like rolling the dough out into balls and dropping them in the big pot and watching them swell up."

The old Irish cook, Sarah, gave a hearty laugh and interrupted, "Sure you can, child. I'll show you how to roll out pie dough, too. One day, you'll be able to cook the whole meal and I can sit and rest these old feet. That Lucinda shore ain't a lot of help."

"Shut your mouth, old woman," Lucinda said under her breath. "I've already taught this here child to mop, sweep and make beds as well as any high-class hotel maid, and she helps do all the other housekeeping chores."

Abby smiled at the compliment Lucinda had given her, but she liked cooking better than cleaning house. Lucinda never spoke harshly or used unkind words when she didn't do something right. Abby's childhood was not a normal one, but with Lucinda, the old Irish cook and her school teachers, she was maturing into an educated young lady.

As Abby moved around her mama's room, memories of living in a log cabin at the edge of town came to mind. Her papa was one of the local doctors in San Francisco. One day he and several other doctors were called out to the gold mines where an explosion had taken place. Months passed but he never returned home. Several men said that they had seen him enter the mine before another explosion filled the entrance with debris.

At the age of three, Abby was too young to remember him. Hearing her mama's voice brought her back to the present.

"Abby," her mama's voice raspy, "move up closer to me." She patted the mattress in front of her daughter. She was so weak that it took all of her strength to speak.

"I'm here, Mama," Abby replied softly, happy to see that she was awake and calling to her. She had been confined to bed for nearly two weeks, and it was rare that she spoke or even opened her heavy eyelids.

"Child, you know I'm not going to get better—this time," her mama said so softly that Abby could hardly make out her words. "I have been lying here thinking about you after I leave this old world. Please take my necklace, my locket. I want you to have it."

Abby slid the necklace from around her mama's neck and placed it on hers. She had always admired this piece of jewelry and wanted many times to peek at the portraits inside the locket, but her mama kept it hidden down the front of her dress. She had only seen the tiny pictures inside it once.

"Listen closely to what I have to say." Bella placed her frail fingers on Abby's rosy lips so she wouldn't speak. "Promise me you'll do as I say. I want to go in peace, knowing that you won't live the same kind of life I have." She closed her eyes for a long time. Abby waited for several long minutes thinking that she may have already slipped away, but slowly she batted her eyes open. After a long coughing spell, she cleared her throat and continued with her plea.

"I don't want you to stay here. This place is not safe

for a lovely like you. Lucinda won't be able to keep the men downstairs away from you, even if she tries." Her words trailed off. "You understand what I'm saying to you?"

Abby nodded. With near panic, she responded. "But, Mama, I don't have any money to leave, and I wouldn't know where to go." This request was so hard to believe. Her mama never let her go anywhere, and now she was instructing her to leave the only home she had ever known.

"Look there," her mama pointed a weak, shaky finger toward an oak wardrobe against the wall. "Open the door and look under a loose board on the bottom. There's a sock filled with paper money and a few gold nuggets that you can take to the land office and cash in."

Abby hurried to the wardrobe and did as her mama instructed. She placed the small woolen sock on her mama's stomach. Her mama clutched the sock and placed it in her daughter's hands.

"Take this and hide it, and don't let anyone know that you have money, especially Lucinda. Promise me!" A coughing fit overtook her for a few minutes, and Abby offered her water to drink. She wet a soft cloth and wiped her mama's mouth and chin.

"Whatever you say, Mama, but you'll be better with rest and good food. Please don't leave me." Tears trailed down her cheeks as she laid her head on her mama's chest. "Please, please don't leave me."

Bella pushed on Abby's shoulders to make her sit up. "Child, I don't want to leave you, but I'm so weary." Her mother's voice trembled as she rubbed her hand over Abby's head. "I know you'll be all right once I'm laid to rest." Abby continued to weep. "Listen now, this is important. Go see Jackson Waters. He'll take care of you. He'll make sure you leave this town. Understand?"

"No Mama, I don't understand. Who is he? Where is he?" Abby asked, not sure who this man was to her mama. She had never heard the man's name before.

"Ask anyone. Everybody knows him. He's a good man and I want you to do whatever he tells you," she said softly. "Abby," her voice was only a whisper. She closed her eyes for the last time, leaving Abby and the old world behind.

"Mama, Mama, please—don't leave me." Abby's cries fell on deaf ears until Lucinda rushed into the room.

"Oh dear," the old woman said as she moved Abby off the bed and covered the frail body of her dear friend and boss lady.

"Come, child. Let's go downstairs. I've got to send for the doctor and the undertaker's wagon. We know that your mama has suffered for a long while. We're gonna miss her, but she is not in any more pain," Lucinda said, as she wiped her eyes with a hanky that she'd pulled from her sleeve.

After the doctor and undertaker left the saloon, Abby

slowly climbed the stairs to her room. Crying until her nose and eyes were red and swollen, she poured water in a basin, laid a cold cloth on her face and stretched out on the bed. As she lay staring at the old ceiling, she felt the locket lying heavy on her chest. She sat up and opened it to see a picture of a lovely, young girl and a handsome man—her parents, both gone now. "Oh mama, papa."

Abby body's shook from the realization that her mama was gone, and she needed to make plans to leave the saloon that had been her home most of her life. Abby's eyes took in the whole room seeing it differently now that she was alone. As long as her mama was alive Abby felt safe, but now, her mama's last words made her afraid. She had never liked living in the saloon, but Mama said that she couldn't support them working anywhere else.

Abby wished that she could remember living in their small cabin at the edge of town where her mama took in washing and ironing. She did remember a big fire and that later they had no place to live. As she got older she was told that after the fire, many of her mama's customers had left the city.

With no roof over their head and no customers to do their washing and ironing, she had no way to earn money for herself and a small child. So, her mama gathered their meager belongings and strode to the back door of The Red Dog Saloon where she pleaded for a job. She cooked and helped clean the big two-story building. After months of slaving away, cooking and mopping floors, her mama began working in the loud, rowdy saloon where she could make a better living.

Shaking her head to erase the sad childhood she'd endured, Abby pulled herself together to take care of business. She had cared for her dying mama for weeks, and now at the age of eighteen, it was time to take care of herself.

"You can do what needs to be done," she said aloud to herself. She walked over to her mirror and re-plaited her golden-blonde hair. Everyone said that she was a pretty little thing, a mirror image of her mama, but she never thought too much about her appearance.

Abby knew that she wasn't expected to do anything today, but it was a nice afternoon and there was no reason to delay taking care of business. Before putting on one of her nicer calico dresses, she tucked the sock of money under her soft corset and tied it as tight as she could. She slid her small feet into her brown boots and grabbed her mama's pretty shawl off the hook by the door. Tears flooded her eyes as she wrapped the shawl around her shoulders and breathed in her mama's scent.

Abby's first stop—visit the undertaker who would take care of her mama's burial. She didn't want to leave everything up to Lucinda. Her mama's resting place was her responsibility. While she was out, she would stop at the dry goods store and purchase a black piece of material that she would wrap around her arm. She didn't have the time or the money to have a new black dress made to wear while she was in mourning. The black binding would have to do.

With the hot afternoon summer sun beating down on her face, she felt strange being out of the saloon without a chaperone. Abby could feel many eyes on her as she made her way to the undertaker's door. After discussing arrangements for the burial and expense of the coffin with Mr. Whitney, the old bony undertaker, she felt better because he was so kind.

"Bella, that's what I called your mama, helped me once when no one else would, and I have never forgotten her kindness." He glanced back over his thin shoulder and whispered to her that they would call her bill paid in full. Abby smiled and gave him a nod. After settling on the time for the burial the next day, she asked Mr. Whitney if he knew Jackson Waters.

"Sure do," he said. "Everybody knows Mr. Jack. That's what we old-timers call him. He's the banker man at the First Bank of San Francisco."

How or why would her mama know a banker? Maybe he was one of her 'customers,' as she heard some of the ladies refer to the men who came up to their rooms. She had never asked her mama what she did with the men who visited with her. Now, she wished she had.

Being careful not to make eye contact with any of the rough men on the boardwalk, she wished she had remembered to put on her bonnet. As she passed people, several young men whistled and pretended to fall in behind her. She hurried down the boardwalk being careful to avoid getting shoved into the muddy street.

After arriving at the bank building with its tall ceilings and shiny floors, she wondered why her mama had never brought her to this establishment before. It was the fanciest place she had ever seen with its big doors and tall mirrors on the wall.

Abby was greeted by a nice young man who wore wire-rimmed glasses and a tie that looked like it might choke him. He pulled on his collar and said," How may I help you, Miss?" She smiled and said that she would like to speak with Mr. Jackson Waters.

Clicking his heels together, he asked, "Whom shall I say is requesting to speak with him?" If Abby had not been so sad, she would have laughed at the young man. She had read that military men and royal servants clicked their heels together.

"My name is Abby Mills. My mama, Isabella Mills, told me to call on him."

The young man raised his eyebrows when he heard the name, Isabella Mills, but requested that she take a seat in one of the cushioned chairs while he checked to see if Mr. Waters was available. He walked away like he had a board pushed up under the back of his blue coat. As Abby waited, her insides trembled. Lucinda would probably have a fit if she knew that Abby had left the saloon alone with the intentions of visiting a total stranger, a man at that. Abby waited and watched the other customers come and go. Maybe Mr. Waters didn't want to see her. She didn't know how much longer she could contain her tears. Watching her mama die was the hardest thing she had ever done.

After what seemed like an eternity, a tall, nice-looking gentleman with thinning gray hair hurried across the shiny floor. He sported a smile on his clean-shaven face.

"I'm so sorry to have kept you waiting so long. Please come into my office where we can speak privately. I'm so sorry to learn of Bella's death." He took her arm and led her into a spacious office with big glass windows that faced the front of the building. The bright afternoon sun shone into the office. He immediately lowered the shade and asked if that was better.

"Yes," she responded softly as she wiped at her eyes with a clean hanky. Being in a strange building with a total stranger who was going to help make plans for her future was unsettling. She wished her mama had talked to her about this man before she became so ill.

Mr. Waters assisted Abby into a chair while he stood near the side of his desk, an arm's length away from her. The tall professional man fiddled with his watch. Did she make him nervous?

"May I send for a glass of water while you tell me what I can do for you today, Miss Mills?"

"Yes, thank you. Water would be nice." Abby needed time to collect her thoughts now that she had met Mr. Waters.

Mr. Waters walked to the door, summoned a young clerk, and asked for a pitcher of water. As they waited, she surveyed the room and saw a picture of a young man and a handsome boy hanging on the wall. "Is that you and your son, Mr. Waters?" Abby asked.

"No, that young man is my nephew. That picture was taken the day after we discovered gold."

Abby studied the picture. "I remember seeing him at school. He was many grades ahead of me, but I saw him on the playground."

A pretty young lady carried a pitcher of cold water and two glasses and placed them on Mr. Waters' desk. She smiled at Abby and left the office.

Abby drank the water and set the glass on the desk. She swallowed and cleared her throat. Trying hard not to show how nervous she felt, she folded both of her hands together and finally spoke.

"Mr. Waters, I don't know what you can do for me. You see, this morning my mama was sick. She told me to come see you. Your name was one of the last things she said to me. She demanded that I leave town and go somewhere safe. Mama said you could help me. Were you and Mama good friends, Mr. Waters? I never heard your name before today." Abby was satisfied that she had gotten all the words out without crying.

"Yes, we were. I knew your mama years before I struck it rich. Way before I built this bank," he said as he waved his hand around the room. "I had a sawmill business up the river with my young nephew. After I made it *big,* as the old miners remind me all the time, I tried several times to give your mama money to take you and get out of this rough town, but she wouldn't hear of it. Your mama was a stubborn woman. She was determined to make her own way. Besides that, she was waiting for your pa to return. She loved him very much."

"I don't remember him at all. Mama never would talk to me about him," she said as she touched the locket that she was now wearing. Her eyes clouded with tears.

"I met your pa, a young doctor, the first week he arrived in town. He was a fine man. Soon, your folks met and married. They were a happily married couple until he rode up into the hills to care for a crew of men who had been in a bad mining accident. He never came back. Your mama sent men to search for him at the mining camps, but they always returned without information about his whereabouts."

"I wish I had some memory of him. All I have is this small picture in my locket." She held it up for him to see. "I always wanted to know him."

Mr. Waters cleared his throat and gave Abby a weak smile. "Well, I think you were too young to remember. I won't mention him again, but I may be able to help you escape from here if you are willing to live in wide-open spaces away from big cities."

Abby couldn't believe what this man had said. If she

could move out of a rat-infested building, away from nasty tobacco smoke, loud music and rowdy men—that would be a dream come true.

"I would love to live where I could be outside, breathe fresh air and roam freely." Being able to walk outside whenever she wanted certainly was a wonderful thought. "Luc, I mean Lucinda and Mama would never allow me out of the saloon except to go to school. I never had any freedom or even a friend," she said as she hung her head.

"My gracious child, how old are you now?"

"I'm not a child any longer. I just had my eighteenth birthday, but Lucinda told me to say I was fourteen if anyone questioned my age. She made me wear a…well, never mind, and I wore my hair in pigtails. When I wasn't helping her or the cook, I stayed in my room reading. My teachers always kept me supplied with books to read at home."

"Yes, I can see that was a good idea that Lucinda had to protect you."

***

Jackson Waters peered at Abby from her head to her toes and studied her crystal green eyes. This was a lovely girl with a sweet disposition. She would be perfect for what he had in mind.

"Listen to me, child. I'm sure your mama sent you to me because she knew that I would take care of you. She wanted you to have my protection. I'm willing to take

17

on the task of caring for you until we can make some plans. First thing, you're not to go back to the saloon." He stood and rounded the large oak desk. "I have a big house with a live-in housekeeper and you'll come and stay at my home until we finalize a plan that I am thinking about now."

Abby's head jerked up and she stared at the stranger standing in front of her. "You can't be serious, Mr. Waters. I don't know you at all. How do I know I will be safer at your place than the saloon?"

"For one thing, Miss Mills, every man in San Francisco knows that Bella has passed and that she had a lovely daughter living upstairs in that establishment. Bella talked about you, but I had forgotten that you had grown up. I'm sure a few of the wealthy men of San Francisco will call on Lucinda and offer to take care of you, but that is not going to happen. Your keeper, Lucinda, I am certain, will be no help to you. I'm sure she'll be more than happy to let some man take you off her hands for a hefty price."

"Oh my goodness, I guess that's the reason Mama instructed me to look you up and not trust Lucinda. I have some money, but she told me not to tell her."

Jackson Waters was sure he had the ideal place to send this beautiful girl. His nephew, Mason, had just sent him a letter asking for his help, and heaven help him, he had no idea how he was going to fulfill his request, until now.

"Miss Mills, may I call you Abby?"

"Please do. You are the only person to ever call me Miss Mills," Abby said smiling. She had hardly ever spoken with anyone except Lucinda, her mama and the school teacher. She wasn't allowed to speak with any of the men in the saloon or on the street.

"Yes, of course, Abby. Please give me a few minutes and I will take you to my home where my housekeeper, Roberta, will care for you. After you've rested, I'll tell you what I think my best plan for your future might be."

## Chapter 2

"What?" Abby said much too loud. "You want me to become a mail-order bride?" Was this Mr. Waters' plan for her future? Did he want to send her to a foreign land to marry someone she had never met?

"No, no, child. It's not like that at all."

"Well, it sure sounds like it. I've read where women travel miles to marry total strangers. Most of the time, those women were desperate and had no other choice." Abby placed her hand over her heart and felt it beating as if she had just run a race.

"Of course, that is not *your* case, but I have a letter here in my hand," Jackson said as he held up a sheet of paper and waved it in the air. "This is from Mason, my nephew. He worked with me at the sawmill when we struck gold. While he was growing up and attending school, he continued to work with me at the saw mill and later managed the whole thing when I opened my bank. He never liked living here, so after a year of searching for just the right property for a cattle ranch, he moved to Northern California, near the border of Oregon. He has been away from San Francisco for two years and he's ready to settle down with a wife and have a family. Now sit back down and listen to the letter that he wrote me requesting my help."

After Abby's breathing had returned to normal and she was seated in a comfortable chair, he began reading the letter.

*Dear Uncle Jack,*

*I am sorry to have let so much time go by without writing. I have been busy with building the ranch house and all the corrals, gates and new fences that had to be put up or repaired. The house is completed but needs furniture, oil lamps, and many other things. I haven't had time until now to make a list for you to purchase much-needed items for me. Mostly I want a big four-poster bed.*

*My cattle arrived and they're a healthy-looking bunch. Most of the animals made the trip up from Mexico. Jed, the foreman of the drive, said I lost about fifty head. I'm waiting for twenty horses to arrive soon from a horse ranch about fifty miles away. I am in need of a few more hard-working men. If you know of any who are willing to work, I'm hiring and will pay a decent wage. They could come on the freight wagons when you ship my items and lumber that I have on the enclosed list.*

*I have a more personal request. I would like for you to place a notice in the paper for a mail-order bride for me. I'm lonely to the point that Cactus Flower, the old Indian woman who works for me, is beginning to look good, even though she only has one big tooth in her mouth and she wears an eighteen-inch blade strapped to her leg for protection. I have never seen her without it.*

*I want a mature girl that can read, write, cook, sew, and clean. I don't wish for a socialite who requires servants. I don't need someone to take care of, but a willing partner who will help me with the house, a small garden and the smaller farm animals.*

*The trading post and surrounding area are growing. Our trading post is carrying many staple goods. You might want to start shipping items up here to Mr. Peterson. I will speak to him for you. Everyone here needs a little of everything. We have a church service that's held in the back of Peterson's store once a month when the traveling minister passes this way.*

*Please fulfill my list as soon as possible and choose wisely on my bride-to-be. I would like someone who is easy on the eye.*

*Your nephew*

*Mason*

"Someone who is easy on the eye; what does he mean?" Abby asked, a line forming between her brows.

Jackson tossed his head back and laughed at her confusion. "Abby dear, he is requesting a pretty girl, just like you. Yes sir, he will be very pleased with you."

"Wait! Please, Mr. Waters. I haven't agreed to go off into the wilderness with a man I haven't met. I don't know much about marriage, but I would think a man and woman would have to know each other. I know I must get out of this town, but please don't ask me to rush into marriage with a total stranger."

"Child, by the time you get ready to leave, I can assure you that Mason, my nephew, will not be a stranger to you. Roberta, my housekeeper, and I will tell you all about him. He's a good Christian man who takes care of his property, his animals and will care deeply for you in time." He smiled at her, then walked over and pulled the cord on the drapery. Roberta appeared shortly afterwards with a tray of brandy, a few cigars, and a cup of tea.

After Roberta had set the tray on a side table, she took the cup of tea and served it to Abby.

"Roberta, I read Mason's letter to Abby. Why don't you tell her what you know about my nephew?" Mr. Waters walked to the fireplace, placed a slim stick of wood in the fire and lit a cigar before he sat down.

"Oh, honey, they don't come any finer than Mason. He was always a good boy, but he's an extraordinary man now. Mason loves the Lord and will not hit a lick of work on Sundays. He said that Sunday is the Lord's Day and it was made for worship, resting or going fishing. Everyone who knows Mason respects him. And he's one handsome devil, if I do say so myself." She grinned at Mr. Waters, who gave her a wink that showed that he appreciated what she said about his nephew.

Mr. Waters said, "Mason left San Francisco because of the lifestyle here. This town has always been too wild for him. He enjoys wide-open spaces, and with all these people coming from all parts of the world to pan for gold, he moved away. I'm Mason's only kin ever since he was a young boy. His mother, my beloved sister, died in a boating accident. His parents went on a picnic on the river, but on their return trip home, the current was too rough for Murray to handle. Murray was my brother-in-law. Nice man but not an outdoorsman. He was a school teacher. Well, the boat capsized and my sister drowned. Later Murray took his own life. It was a sad time for all of us. I brought Mason down the river with me and taught him how to help with the sawmill business. He was nine at the time."

"Why wasn't he on the outing with his folks?" Abby asked.

"From what I remember, he had been sick with a cold and my sister didn't want him to be in the wind and possibly get wet, so he stayed home and played with a friend. I guess that was a blessing. Mason has been with me ever since, and I have never regretted taking him in." Mr. Waters cleared his throat. "Abby, my nephew is now five and twenty. As you heard from his letter, he's ready to settle down and have a family. I would never send you to marry Mason if I didn't think he was a good, respectable man who, in time, will grow to love and care deeply for you. I feel that you will like him, too." He took a sip of his brandy while glancing at Roberta. She gave him a nod to continue.

"One more important thing about my nephew. He's a wealthy young man, but he doesn't brag or tell anyone about his wealth. He likes nice, simple things. I know he will be generous with you if you hold up your end of the marriage bargain."

"Marriage bargain?" She had read stories in her romance books about men and women making bargains to marry, but the brides were usually desperate and had no other choice to survive. She guessed her situation was much the same as some of those ladies she had read about.

"Do I have to sign a paper agreeing to do certain things with or for your nephew?" She was confused because she didn't hear anything about a bargain in his letter.

"Well, I'll write to Mason that you've agreed to be his wife, but you would like to have a period of time to adjust to each other. I'll explain that you would need time to get to know him better before the marriage is consummated. You are a young woman who has never been around men or even courted by one. I am sure he will agree to the terms."

Abby sat staring across the room at Mr. Waters and thought she liked this part of the marriage agreement, but would his nephew want to wait until she made her decision?

"Abby, do you know what consummate a marriage means?"

Abby's head jerked up, and she glared at the older gentleman. She felt her face flame from embarrassment. She was young and innocent, but did he think she was a dimwit that had her head in the sand while living in a saloon? "Mr. Waters, I am educated and I know all about what takes place between a man and woman," she replied in a soft whisper. She peered down at her hands and hoped that he wouldn't notice how uncomfortable she felt.

"Move on, Jackson, to another subject," Roberta said, trying to hold her laughter in check.

Jackson cleared his throat and continued. "As he has written in this letter, he desires a woman who can cook. Can you cook?" he asked, his head tilted slightly.

"Yes," Abby answered. "I enjoy cooking very much. Lucinda let me help cook in the kitchen most evenings. I love to bake pies. Would you like for me to bake one for dinner?"

"No, that won't be necessary," he replied with a grin.

Mr. Waters glanced at a piece of paper with a list on it. Abby had not noticed him holding it before. "What about keeping a house clean? Oh, yes, you did say you helped the housekeeper with mopping and cleaning the saloon."

"Yes, that's right and I washed all of my own clothes. Mama had a lady come and get her clothes once a week and wash and iron her pretty things."

"Why didn't the lady do your things for you?" Roberta interrupted.

"I don't rightly know. Ever since I was a little tyke, I washed my things in a large tub on the back porch of the saloon and hung them on a line to dry in good weather."

"I can tell you weren't spoiled," Mr. Waters said through tightened lips. "One more thing and I believe I will know all about you and your ability to be the perfect bride for my nephew. Can you sew?"

Abby liked this man. She had liked him since their very first conversation. "Yes, I can sew. I made all my school clothes and most of my other items. I enjoy embroidery, but I didn't have money to purchase the threads. I like to crochet, too."

"Well, Roberta, what do you think about Miss Abby being Mason's mail-order-bride?"

"Perfect, she's just perfect. We could look San Francisco over and never find a more perfect mate for him." Roberta took Abby's hands and pulled her out of the chair. "Come, child. It's time for you to go to bed. You've had a long, sad day."

"Wait, I do have another question for Mr. Waters. Why is it important that I marry your nephew? Why can't I live on his ranch and get to know him first?"

"Well, it would not be proper for you to live alone with Mason without a chaperone. The few ladies in the village would never welcome you into their homes. You would be treated like an outcast, a lady without morals," Roberta explained.

Mr. Waters said, "Abby, you've been shunned enough in your life. I'm sure your mama knew that I would protect you like you were my own daughter. Bella wanted the best for you. Mason and I will see that you have everything you need."

"Please, I don't want to be a burden to anyone. I have some money that Mama had hidden away, but my things are upstairs in my room at the saloon. I'll need to go, pack and tell Lucinda my plans."

"No, it's not safe for you to return or to be walking these streets alone. My man, Joseph, will retrieve your items. If this Lucinda doesn't help him gather your things, he'll collect them all by himself. He's a resourceful man," he said with a chuckle.

Roberta led Abby out of the large parlor up the stairs to her room. "Tomorrow, we'll go to the store and pick you out some ready-made dresses and other things. You must have a bride's trousseau."

"I thought I needed to save my money for travel," Abby said, still not understanding how wealthy her groom-to-be was.

"One thing you will never have to worry your pretty head about is money. We'll get everything you need and Mr. Waters will take care of the expense. I will

return in a few minutes to help you prepare for bed."
Roberta shut the door quietly, leaving Abby alone to
ponder her new future.

# Chapter 3

Abby covered another yawn after getting settled into Mr. Waters' lovely home at the end of Main Street. So much had happened in a short period of time. Her mama had been ill for weeks, but she had always recovered and returned to work. This last time her illness was more critical as she fought to breathe with bouts of coughing that racked her frail body.

Abby felt the smoked-filled saloon was the reason her mama had developed weak lungs and had a hard time breathing. Each time the doctor came, he always left with a grim expression on his face and offered no words of encouragement. "Stay with her, child." Wiping his mouth with a dirty rag, he said, "Keep her comfortable" as the door closed. Abby never left her mama's side, day and night for two weeks until she finally took her last breath.

With the plans for her mama's funeral all set for the next morning, Abby allowed Roberta to help her prepare for bed. Before she retired, she made a list of her belongings that Joseph needed to get and items of her mama's that she treasured from the saloon.

As she stretched her exhausted body under the beautiful light green quilt that covered the double bed, Roberta carried something dark in her arms. "Mr. Waters would like for you to wear this dress to the funeral along with this hat and veil." She held it up and glanced at Abby. "He thinks it will be better for you if the men of the city don't see how lovely you truly are. Most of them have only heard about you from gossip.

"Did you know my mama?" Abby asked as she nestled under the quilt.

"No, not personally, but Mr. Waters often spoke about her and how hard she worked to support herself and you. Your mama was a good woman. He recalled how your mama worked alongside the doctors when the cholera epidemic hit the city. It was a blessing that she didn't get the disease. He said that she helped many people in this town before the gold rush, even though she worked hard to earn her money." Roberta hung the black dress up and smiled at Abby. "You rest now, and I will help you dress in the morning for the burial." Roberta moved toward the door, blew out the lantern and softly closed the door.

When Abby opened her eyes the next morning, she felt like she was in a beautiful dream. The large bed was big enough for three people and the draperies looked like some she had seen in a storybook. The dark green velvet material with fringe running down the sides hung from the ceiling to the floor. Soft matching rugs were scattered everywhere in the room. A small fire was built in the fireplace to help take the chill out of the air. As she lay looking at the ceiling, she wondered who else might live in this big lovely mansion with Mr. Waters.

Roberta knocked on her door and opened it immediately, not giving her time to answer. "Good morning, Abby. I let you sleep as long as I could, but you must get ready for the funeral. I brought you a breakfast tray with hot tea instead of coffee. I just guessed which one you would rather have, but if you want some coffee, I will fetch it for you."

"Tea sounds grand. I don't remember when I have slept so soundly. Even the street noises didn't keep me awake," Abby replied as she looked at the attractive housekeeper. She had a smooth complexion, dark eyes and dark brown hair plaited like a crown around the back of her head, so different from her mama and the other ladies at the saloon.

"I understand you have been sitting with your mama for weeks without much sleep. You needed to get a good night rest. Now hurry and eat so I can help you into this lovely black dress. When you're away from the city, you won't need to wear black all the time, unless you want too."

As Roberta prepared to leave the room, Abby asked, "How long have you worked for Mr. Waters?"

"Well, let's see. I believe I have been here for nearly fifteen years. My husband died and my grown children live far away. Jackson needed someone to help care for his nephew. You know, with cooking and cleaning and overseeing Mason with his school work. Several years later after they struck it rich, Jackson built this nice house. About that time, his nephew didn't need me anymore, but Jackson did. I moved in with several other servants and I'm still here. Jackson and I have become great friends and he doesn't treat me like a servant. He shares his daily life with me at dinner each night. I enjoy being here." Roberta smiled and left the room while Abby sat on the side of the bed eating toast and sipping hot tea.

Mr. Waters stood next to Abby at the funeral. The traveling minister, who was as thin as an old willow tree, had a long gray pigtail hanging down his back. He stood on the mound of dirt in front of the coffin. He was wearing a dark brown suit that looked to be about two sizes too large for his slim frame. Towering over the unexpected large crowd, the minister waited for everyone to settle down before he began his opening prayer.

As his words flowed over the group, Abby was surprised at the number of miners, young and old, and businessmen who had taken time away from their shops. She was sure there were at least a hundred or more men dressed in their dark blue overalls and work boots. A few ladies from the local orphanage circled the area where the coffin was being lowered. A young lady, whom Abby had never met, stepped forward and sang a Christian hymn, "Thy Love's Unbounded". The words flowed out over the crowd as tears streamed freely down her face.

As a fresh flower was placed in her hand, she noticed that Mr. Waters held one, too. He tossed it on the coffin, so Abby followed with her flower and tossed it on the coffin as it was being lowered into the ground. She had never attended a funeral before. She was only beginning to realize how closely she had been protected and closed off from the outside world. Maybe if she had been allowed to go to church, she would have heard the hymn that the young girl was singing over her mama's grave.

Lucinda, dressed in a long old black dress that dipped in the front and rode high on her backside, rushed over and hugged Abby. She grasped her arm as if to lead her away from the crowd. Mr. Waters intervened and stood between Abby and the old housekeeper.

"Miss Abby will be not be returning to her room, Lucinda. She's under my protection now and I'll see to her care."

Lucinda sucked in her breath and blew out a big huff. "What's the meaning of this, old man? I have practically raised this child. Get out of my way. This girl is like a daughter to me. Abby, tell this old goat that you're going home with me."

Tears filled Abby's eyes as she looked at the older woman who had been the closest thing to a friend she had over the years. "Please, Luc. Try to understand that I'm not returning to the saloon. Mama's last wish was for me to seek Mr. Waters' help. I'll be leaving San Francisco soon. Thank you for all of your help over the years. I shall always remember your kindness to me."

"What'd you say, girl? You can't just up and leave me. You owe me!" Lucinda shrieked. She whirled around Mr. Waters and grabbed Abby's arm, pulling her away.

Mr. Waters raised his hand, and before Lucinda knew what was happening to her, she was lifted off the ground and escorted away from the gravesite by two big, burly men. They continued carrying her away as she squawked and demanded that Abby come and pay off her debt. She screamed that she had cared for her and now it was time for her to be repaid.

Abby was in total shock at Lucinda's attitude and cruel words. "I'm sorry," Abby whispered to Mr. Waters. "I didn't know that I owed her anything. I worked hard in the saloon, washing, mopping, and cleaning all the time. Lucinda didn't love me, but she was kind and taught me many things. Now, I have a feeling she wants me to do a different kind of job."

"I'm afraid you are right, my dear, which is the reason you aren't going back anywhere near that place again. Oh my, look, Abby." Abby glanced where Mr. Waters was pointing. An older man held his hat out in front of all the men. They were placing money into his old floppy hat.

"What's he going to do with that money?"

"It's for you. Please accept it. The men want to help take care of Bella's child." Mr. Waters smiled sheepishly down at her.

In shocked awe, she watched old and young men alike, standing with their heads bowed and placing money into the older man's hat. She headed slowly over to the line of men, graciously shook each hand and thanked them for coming. The men smiled, nodded and walked out of the cemetery. The man that had collected the money approached Abby and said how sorry he and the men were about Bella's passing. He offered her the cash, and with tears running down her face hidden behind the thin black veil, she accepted it with heartfelt thanks.

Abby gave the money to Mr. Waters as they made their way back to his carriage. Glancing back at the grave one more time, she saw three of the painted ladies that worked at the saloon huddled together.

"I'll be right back, Mr. Waters." She strolled over to the ladies. Suzie, the youngest girl, broke away from the group and hurried over to Abby. She took her hands and then dropped them as if she was being rude.

"Miss Abby, I'm so sorry about your mama, Miss Bella. She was good to me, in her own way, but she wouldn't allow me to play with you, much less speak to you. We're about the same age and I always wanted to be your friend, but that witch, Lucinda, said that I was 'tainted.'"

"Tainted?" Abby said. "What did she mean?"

Suzie looked toward the other ladies who were signaling with their heads for her to come along. "You know, I had to live upstairs with the other ladies. I never wanted to do it, but she would have put me in the streets. I've got to go now, but I wanted to say that I'm sorry. Good-bye." Suzie raced away. Abby watched as the ladies turned and headed out of the cemetery.

Wiping tears from her eyes, Abby joined Mr. Waters back at his carriage.

"Did you know that young lady?" Mr. Waters asked.

"No, but I saw her many times in the kitchen. She said that my mama wouldn't let her come near me, but she had always wanted to be my friend. Suzie had to be about ten when she came to live at the saloon. I just thought that she didn't like me. I can't believe Mama kept me from having a playmate. She knew how lonely I was."

As the big carriage drove through the muddy streets that had been lined with wide boards to keep the wagon wheels from getting stuck, Mr. Waters asked Abby, "Are you hungry?"

"No, thank you. I would like to return to your home and lie down. I'm sure Miss Roberta will feed me later."

# Chapter 4

Three weeks passed, and Mr. Waters had the supplies ready to be carried to Mason's ranch near a trading post called Eagle's Station. There would be four freight wagons fully packed on the trip. Each wagon would be pulled by six sturdy mules because of the load they carried. Jackson had purchased new furnishings for Mason's house.

There were bed frames, stuffed mattresses, a table and chairs, large wooden tubs, and oil lamps. Lovely china was wrapped and packed in barrels. He purchased all types of hardware that were used on a ranch—hoes, pitchforks and crowbars. These items would be packed on two wagons with wire for fences and ponderosa pine lumber that would be used for buildings and red cedar for making canoes and small boats.

Another wagon would carry everything from sewing

supplies to all types of farming equipment to help with items to sell at the trading post. Positioned on the front of one of the freight wagons was a small cavalry tent for Abby's sleeping arrangement and her trunk of clothes, blankets, pillows and personal items. The men who traveled on the trip would sleep under the wagons or around the campfire.

Mr. Waters had hired three men to work on Mason's one hundred-acre ranch. There would be four drivers for the wagons, a cook and a young wrangler to take care of the animals. This would provide plenty of men to help protect Abby and the supplies. Many people knew that Mr. Waters had valuable cargo on this freight wagon train, plus Bella's pretty young daughter. Each man would be issued a handgun and a rifle, and the men would be required to help stand guard at night.

Mr. Waters had made arrangements with Zeke Davies to be the trail master, and he made him responsible for seeing that Mason's bride-to-be would arrive safe and sound.

"I'll protect her just like she was my own young'un, you can bet your life on that," Zeke stated, as he spit a chew of tobacco juice about three feet away from where they stood. Zeke was an older man who stood about five-foot-five inches tall and had arms like short logs. Even with most of his teeth missing, he had a ready smile for everyone.

"If any of the men get out of line with her—in any way, give them a few dollars and send them on their way," Waters said. "She's a nice girl and she's to be treated with respect. Miss Mills is not spoiled or lazy. I'm sure she will help any way she can. You drive the wagon that has her tent on it."

"The men are all ready to go and the mules are in good shape. Good idea of yours to take along two extras. You never know what can happen on the trail with animals."

"Abby will be ready at daylight to move out. See you in the morning," Jackson said as he shook the old trail master's hand.

## Chapter 5

After a tearful goodbye to Roberta, Abby came out of the house with a small carpetbag. She stopped in her tracks on the walkway of Mr. Waters' lovely home. Mr. Waters was standing at the door of his smaller carriage with his mouth wide open. "What in the blazes are you wearing? A nice girl like you don't wear such—" He stumbled over the right words to say. Abby could not believe that this sweet man had shouted at her.

"I'm wearing trousers, sir," she said, embarrassed that he was gawking at her from her head to her new western boots.

"I can see what you're wearing, but why are you dressed in those . . . things?" he demanded. Before Abby could answer, Roberta dashed out the door and stood in front of her, preparing to do battle with her dear friend and boss.

"I instructed Abby to wear the pants. They are so much better for traveling with all those men. She will be climbing up and down, on and off those big wagons and they are so much more practical for…just everything. Abby has several pair and I insist that you allow her to wear them." Roberta pulled Abby out from behind her and pushed her toward the carriage.

Jackson Waters glared at his housekeeper, secretly the love of his life, and finally shook his head. "Thank goodness she'll be out of town and hardly anyone will see her dressed in that garb."

Abby jumped into the carriage without Jackson's help. He stood looking at her as she gave him a big grin. He turned and glanced at Roberta. "You think you've pulled a trick on me, don't you?"

She smiled back at him.

"I'll be home later," he said, with a small chuckle.

***

Abby was sad to be leaving San Francisco, the city where she had grown up and the only home that she had ever known. Her heart was breaking with the knowledge that her mama was gone and she would never be with her again. Roberta had assured her that she would place flowers on her mama's grave.

As she sat on the high wagon bench and breathed the fresh air, she couldn't help but feel a little relief that she wouldn't have to stay shut up in her room all the time.

She could go to sleep without the awful smell of cigar smoke and the loud music all night. Never before had she felt such freedom, having never been outside of the saloon without her mama or Lucinda standing guard. As a young girl, she'd felt like she was in prison.

The young and old men who were on the wagon train were helpful and friendly. She didn't feel afraid of any of the men here like she had of the customers hanging around the saloon. Abby loved listening to Zeke as he called out to the mules that were pulling their wagon. He talked to old Jack, Jenny, Gal, and Gus like they were old friends. Their black ears perked up as their names were called out.

"How to do you know which mule is Jenny or Gus?" Abby asked.

"Well, Missy, each mule has their differences, just like us folks. They look alike mostly, but they sure act different. When you've been around them as much as me, you'll soon learn which one is Gus or Jenny," he snorted with a loud laugh.

"I like your dog," she said, peering down at the ground as a small black and white hound trotted beside the wagon. The pup was running and jumping with his pink tongue hanging out of his mouth.

"The saloon had many cats that roamed around, in and out of all the rooms that kept the mice and other small critters out of the building. I fed the cats on the back porch and had an old favorite tomcat, but I always wanted a dog," Abby said with a sigh.

"Well, I'd be willing to bet that you'll be able to have all the animals you want on Mason's ranch."

"Why don't you allow your dog to ride on the wagon with us? With those short legs, he must be tired of running so fast."

"Well, Missy, he's earning his keep right now. Frisco's nose is close to the ground. He's smelling for bears or mountain lions. If and when he smells something, he'll set off an alarm by barking and running around in a circle."

"My goodness, I would have never guessed that little fellow was so important to this wagon train." Abby looked hard into the thicket of trees and wondered if any wild animals were wandering nearby.

Zeke chewed on his tobacco and spit a stream of juice off the side of the wagon. "Don't fret none. We got Frisco and the men are on guard for ruffians and critters." Zeke kept talking while Abby took in everything he said about their surroundings.

"Frisco is a valuable little critter. His nose has saved many a mule and man on horseback by letting us know that an animal has passed our way or is up ahead of us. At night, I'm going to let him sleep on this wagon in front of your tent. If anything or anybody comes too close, he'll start barking." Zeke glanced at Abby and gave her a little smile.

"Mr. Zeke, you talk like you know Mr. Waters' nephew. Can you tell me something about him?" She held onto the bench and blushed bright pink.

"Now, Missy, you call me Zeke, no mister tagged on," he said, as he gave her a sideways glance.

"To tell you the truth, I've only met him twice. This here is my third trip from San Francisco to his valley. Mason's a big son of a gun. Towers over me, that's for sure," he laughed and choked on his tobacco juice. He wiped his mouth on his sleeve. "Mason is a nice fellow. He's good to his ranch hands and works right along beside them, so I'm told. That speaks a lot for a man."

Abby was silent as she listened to what Zeke had to say. Roberta and Mr. Waters noted that Mason was a good man, and now Zeke said the same thing. Maybe life with him wouldn't be so bad, she thought.

Several long hours passed since the wagon train had left the San Francisco area and was well on the trail to the northern California border when Zeke gave the signal to hold up.

"We'll rest for a spell and have something to eat. The cook will have some grub fixed for us. After you eat something, you might want to rest your bones a bit." Zeke jumped off the wagon and limped along the trail into the bushes.

Once Abby's feet touched the ground, her knees nearly folded under her, and she realized she'd better find some bushes in the opposite direction herself.

Cookie was a man with deep dimples on his face and a round belly. After Abby helped him with the mid-morning meal, she paced alongside the wagons. All the drivers were busy checking their mule's equipment as the young wrangler made sure each one had a fresh bucket of water. They had stopped beside a stream so the men didn't have to use the water in the barrels fastened on the side of the wagons.

She smiled at each man as she strolled down to the stream. Abby picked up several rocks and tossed them in the clear, flowing water. She felt flushed with excitement as she stood alone in the beautiful open wilderness. Alone—without a bodyguard or someone demanding that she hurry back inside and get out of sight.

As she washed her face, an eerie sensation came over her that something or someone was watching her. She had been kneeling at the stream of cold water when she felt a presence behind her. Slowly, she stood and turned around. Leaning up against a tree with his rifle laid over his arm was one of the wagon drivers. He was the young wrangler that Zeke had hired to work on Mason's ranch. His skin was tanned and he had the blackest hair Abby had ever seen on a man. Was he an Indian? He didn't dress like the few she had seen in the past.

"Why are you following me?" she asked the man. It had been foolish of her to walk so far from the campsite. She didn't remember the young man's name. There were so many and she was too excited to listen to Zeke as he called their names out.

"It's not what you think, Miss. Zeke asked me to watch out for you—you know, there are snakes and other critters near the water. Sorry if I made you feel uncomfortable."

"That's all right. I didn't mean to snap at you. What's your name?"

"Name's Chip, Miss."

Abby returned to the wagon and climbed up on it. She was so glad that Roberta had insisted that she wear trousers because they made climbing up and down so much easier. What would Mama think if she saw her daughter in trousers? Well it didn't matter because Mama was gone and she had to stop with the self-pity or she would be weeping like a baby. She climbed into her tent so she could get out of the sun and rest a spell before the wagons started moving again.

The rocking and swaying of the wagon soon lulled Abby into a deep sleep. All she remembered were the creaking sounds of the wheels as they rode over deep ruts and rocks on the trail. As she lay inside the tent, listening to the crickets and frogs, she peeked out at the sky and saw stars and a big moon off in the distance. She leaped up and peered around. The wagons had stopped, so she crawled out of the tent and climbed down. All the men were gathered around a blazing campfire. One of the men was playing a song on a guitar that was pleasant to the ear.

When Abby approached the campfire, the men jumped up and stood when she entered the circle. "Please sit back down. You don't have to be so formal with me out here in the wilderness." She gave the men a sweet smile and they settled back down on their logs and blankets.

"Zeke, I can't believe I slept so long. I slept right past dinner." Abby took a seat on the log next to the old man.

"Yep, you sure did. I didn't have the heart to wake you. Cookie saved a plate of food for you. It's in the chuck wagon."

"I guess I was plain tuckered out. With the excitement of going to a new place with strangers, I guess I haven't been resting well at night. Thanks for letting me nap."

Each day of travel seemed to be the same. Abby had gotten into the routine of rising early to help Cookie prepare breakfast and wash up the tin plates and cups.

The trail from San Francisco to Mason's valley was well used by many people headed away from the overpopulated city. Often they would pass a family in a covered wagon headed to San Francisco. She prayed that they would find a new future and home, but she doubted it. The city had over thirty thousand people already settled in many tent cities. She hoped her new home would bring her freedom and contentment.

## Chapter 6

Mason was concerned over the mail delivery. He hadn't received a response from his uncle for nearly a month. With the weather conditions as nice as they'd been for weeks, he should have received a reply. He was anxious for mail more than ever since he had requested that his uncle seek out a mail-order bride for him. *What a crazy idea. I should have taken the time and traveled back to San Francisco myself and looked for a wife.*

Mason stepped outside on his big front porch that wrapped around his house. The wind was blowing, making the rocking chairs move back and forth. As he stepped off the porch, he decided to saddle his horse, ride into the village and speak with old Peterson at the trading post about the mail.

Mason greeted the old men who stationed themselves on the front porch of the trading post. Old man Peterson was nowhere in sight when he entered the store. He circled the barrels of nails and stood next to several big brooms that had been made by one of the Indians. "Peterson?" Mason called toward the back of the store.

"Hold your horses." A reply came from the top of a ladder in the supply room. In a few minutes, a tall, dark-haired man with wide-set eyes, wearing a white stained apron, appeared. "What's all the hollering about?" he demanded as he stood behind the counter.

"No one's hollering," laughed Mason. "I just called to see if you were here. Figured you had to be around since the door was unlocked," Mason said, as he peered at the pigeon holes that held mail on the wall. Most of the spaces were empty.

"I rode in this afternoon to ask if you knew why there hasn't been any mail lately."

"Yep, I know," he said as he placed a lid on a candy jar. "A few days ago, the young rider who delivers the mail had an accident while crossing the river. Seems something spooked his horse right out from under him and he nearly drowned. He managed to swim to the bank, but his horse floated on down the river with the mail bags tied to the saddle. My guess is if the animal managed to get out of the water, and most likely he did, I'd bet he headed back the way he came."

"Do you know how the rider's doing?"

"He's been staying over at the Old Wise Woman's shack. He swallowed half the river and now he has a bad cough."

Mason was disappointed about the mail, but he was happy to hear that the boy was going to recover.

The Old Wise woman would take good care of him. Everybody in town raved about her methods of treatment and healing ways. Even the white women used her as a midwife. Maybe his future wife would use her too.

"So, Peterson, it looks like we'll have to hire someone else to deliver our mail, both incoming and outgoing."

"Yep. That young boy was upset over losing his job, but it will be awhile before he can travel. His lungs were filled with water, and the Old Wise Woman said he needs time to dry out and get strong again."

"Hopefully, the freight wagons carrying the supplies I ordered from my uncle should be arriving any day. I told Uncle Jackson to send a lot of extra supplies. I thought you might want to sell them in your store. When it gets here, you'll have plenty of items to sell or trade."

"Listen here, Mason." Peterson straightened his backbone and stood stiffly. "I ain't got no money to be purchasing a bunch of supplies from your uncle," he said, taking a dirty rag out of his overalls and wiping at his chin.

"You don't have to buy the items. You'll receive a

commission on each item you sell. The rest of the money will go to my uncle. It's a good business deal for both of you. Don't set the prices too high. Everybody living around here needs many of the items I asked him to send."

"Well then, your uncle has a deal. I'll sell his items." A big grin spread across his face.

Distracted by what he'd learned about the mail Mason nodded toward the door. "Guess I'll be headed on back to the ranch." He turned to go out the door when two young cowpokes came up the steps and entered the doorway, nearly knocking him off his feet.

"Hey, Peterson! Several big freight wagons are headed this way. There are three or four big wagons, and a beautiful gal is sitting on the high bench next to the old driver. Nick says he recognized her, but I ain't so shore about that," Billie said, as he rubbed his chin.

"Who does Nick think the girl is and why is she coming here of all places?" Peterson asked.

"Nick says she's that old madam's daughter, Isabella, who runs The Red Dog Saloon in San Francisco. He didn't see her a lot because she worked upstairs. It's rumored that Isabella, the Queen," he gestured with his eyebrows by lifting them several times, "got sick and died."

Mason stepped closer to the young man who smelled like he had stepped in a pile of horse manure. "How far did you say the freight wagons are from the village? I believe that's my shipment and I'll need to go meet it."

"The wagons are up on the trail about two miles from here. Nick and I stopped and talked with the head driver. Well, we tried to talk, but that small dog guarding that gal nearly ate me alive before one of them other men got a hold of him. That's when we saw the gal up close. I thought at first she was a young boy sitting there, but it weren't. That gal is wearing boy clothes, but she's shore a pretty thing. Golden hair hanging down her back and pretty rosy cheeks, she's a looker, that's for sure."

The two men grabbed a handful of crackers and sauntered into the back where several older men were gathered around a small square table, relaxing in cane-back chairs. Heads were bent down studying the black and red checkerboard. Mason stood watching the two cowboys take tin cups from the pegboard and pour themselves a cup of black coffee.

"Thanks for the information about the mail, Peterson." Placing his black Stetson back on his straight dark hair, he started toward the door. "Since it's so late, we'll bring in the supplies from the freight wagon tomorrow. See you," he said, hanging his head low.

Mason exited the store and headed toward the hitching rail next to his horse. He didn't want to believe what he had just heard from those two dirty cowpokes. The sky had lost its sunshine since he'd gone into the trading post. Dark clouds had formed. It looked like a rainstorm was on the way. As Mason led his horse a little way down the street, he couldn't help but think about the young men's comments.

*Daughter of the queen?* He touched his stomach as it tightened into knots. Vomit rose into his throat and he was sure he was going to eject the sandwich that he had eaten earlier. Surely his uncle wouldn't have sent him a soiled dove for a bride.

Mason remembered Isabella Mills. She and his uncle were old friends. Uncle Jackson frequented the saloon every Saturday night until they struck it rich. Later, Uncle Jackson stopped going to The Red Dog Saloon. When Mason had questioned him about his Saturday night trips, he said it was a nasty habit, and he needed to give it up. Mason was pleased no matter what the reason was.

Mason patted his horse and fed him a piece of sugar out of his palm. He was stalling for time before he mounted his horse and rode out to the freight wagons. Hot and sweaty, he had no idea what he was going to do with the girl. The excitement and anxious moments of waiting for his new mail-order bride left him. Uncle Jackson may have sent her to him, but there was no way in Hades he was going to be tied down to a gal that had been used by every man in San Francisco. Embarrassment and remorse flowed through his tall frame as thoughts flooded his mind. What would others say about them—the lonesome Sunday Boy and the soiled dove.

Mason had gotten the nickname from some of the old men who had offered him a sip of moonshine.

When he turned down the hard liquor and the chewing tobacco and refused to go with the younger ranch hands to the shacks built into the hillside, the oldest man asked if he was a Sunday meeting man. "Sure would be if we had a preacher man to hold services," Mason had firmly replied. Afterward, the old men tagged him with that nickname.

Mounting his horse and riding toward the freight train, Mason prayed that the men were wrong about his new bride. Giving himself a shake, he decided to wait until he met her. No sense jumping to conclusions until he met her in person. His plan had been to chat awhile with the gal, then they would ride straight over to the traveling preacher's room and be married. The old preacher would only be around for two more days, and then he'd be leaving to travel to another small town. There was no way he could take her to his home without having said the words, making her his wife.

## Chapter 7

Mason rode the few miles to the location where the wagons had settled in for the night. The clouds in the sky had darkened, making it seem later than it actually was, and lightning flashed in the distance. He was going to have to hurry before the rain poured down.

After tying his horse to a wagon wheel, he searched for the trail master. Finally, voices came from the other side of the wagons, so he headed to the edge of the group. The old man called Zeke, who Mason had met before, was giving the men instructions on how to prepare the mules and the wagons for the storm. One of the men gave Zeke a nod and he turned to see Mason standing nearby.

"Howdy, boy," Zeke said, wincing. "We just arrived a while ago and I was hoping we could make it out to your place before the storm, but it don't appear we will. We'll just park here for the night, if that is all right with you."

"You chose a good spot. There's a stream nearby with fresh water for the animals. There won't be shelter for them but I'm sure they'll be fine. Tie their pick lines tight, because this lightning will frighten them for sure."

Zeke grinned and motioned Mason to come a little closer. "I guess you want to meet the little gal that we brung you?"

"You're right," he replied with a grin. "Where is she?"

"Come on and I'll get her for you. She's in her tent gathering some of her things." The two men strolled around the big fire and stopped at the first wagon in line. Slowly a body was backing out of the tent. The trim buttocks covered in blue denim scooted out backward on crawling knees. The gal shook her long rope of golden hair back over a shoulder and stood. She reached for her carpetbag and turned to climb down over the wheel of the wagon. With wide eyes like a doe caught in crosshairs, she stopped when she saw the giant of a man standing next to Zeke.

****

Abby's heart trembled as she reached to smooth her blonde hair off her forehead. How she wished she had taken the time to change into one of her new calico dresses. Feeling like a young boy in her shirt and trousers, she stepped on the wheel and jumped down from the wagon. Zeke grabbed her and pulled her close to his side.

"Miss Abby, don't be 'fraid," he whispered in her ear. "This here is Mason Waters, your intended."

"Zeke, I believe I can take the introduction from here." Mason stepped forward and offered his large, calloused hand to Abby.

Trying with all of her might not to show fear of the man that she was going to marry, she peered down and took his extended hand. Her face barely reached the man's chest, and her legs wobbled like they might give way any minute. Just when she thought of hiding behind Zeke, the man returned a tentative smile.

"Are you steady on your feet? Can you walk?" he asked.

"Yes, I think so. I'm a little stiff, but I'm fine now," she said quietly.

*** 

Mason couldn't believe his eyes. This delicate young girl was to be his bride. He had requested a mature woman, not a school girl, but when she looked into his eyes, he felt his heart flip flop.

"With the storm coming so soon, we'd best visit the preacher in the morning and head on out to my place now. That tent of yours won't withstand this storm tonight." Not giving Abby a chance to reply or offer a rebuttal about his plans, he reached up and retrieved her carpetbag.

"Let's go." Mason took her arm and told Zeke he would see him in the morning. "I'll fetch you after we take care of our business with the preacher. Just have breakfast and wait here for me."

Mason led Abby to his big bay horse. "I guess your trousers were a good idea." Before she could respond, he wrapped two large hands around her small waist and lifted her onto his saddle. She settled on the horse and sighed. He could tell she was afraid. Had she ever been on a horse, or was she afraid of him? He tied her carpetbag behind the saddle. "Move up a bit, little one, I'm climbing up behind you."

Mason placed his foot in the stirrup and swung onto the saddle behind Abby. She sucked in her breath while he adjusted the reins and began walking the animal toward the road to his place.

"You'd better breathe and lean back into me if you don't want to faint before we get a mile down the road."

He felt her small body shaking. She hadn't taken time to put on a coat or hat. He was so mesmerized by her beauty that he wasn't thinking straight before he got her on the horse to ride back to his ranch. Mason had asked his uncle to choose a bride that wasn't hard on the eyes, but he never dreamed he would send him a beauty. The thought of her working in a brothel brought him back to reality.

There was a chill in the strong wind that had begun

to blow. He pulled her frail, shaking body back into his chest. "Hold still, gal, or you'll scare my horse." She was shaking so hard that her teeth were chattering.

"Are you cold," he asked.

"No, I'm fine," she said through chattering teeth.

Mason held the reins with one hand and slid off his denim jacket. "Here, wrap this around your shoulders or better yet, place your arms in the sleeves and pull it close."

"I said I'm not cold."

"I know you are cold so wrap up in my jacket."

"I'm not cold and I don't want your coat," Abby yelled into the wind.

"Put this jacket on or I'll stop and put it on you myself." He let out a frustrated breath of air.

Slowly, Abby took the jacket and slipped her arms into the sleeves. He could tell it warmed her. "I'm sorry I forgot my coat and hat. I feel bad taking yours." She whispered softly to him as she snuggled into the jacket.

After about a mile on the trail toward Mason's ranch, which he named Eagle's Nest, large raindrops began falling. "I was hoping we would make it to the ranch before it stormed, but no such luck today. We're only a couple of miles away. We'll be there before you know it." The night sky was as dark as molasses.

The rain came down in sheets with the wind blowing in every direction. The rain was like pellets hitting him and Abby in the face. Mason took off his hat and placed it on her head. She immediately took it off and attempted to give it back to him. "Put it on!" Mason yelled into her ear.

"You've already given me your coat. You need the hat."

Mason took the hat and slapped it back down on her head. "Leave it on or else," he shouted over the thunder.

"Are you going to hit me if I don't," she cried.

"For the love of the saints, woman, keep the hat on!" he shouted, as the rain cascaded down his face.

Water flowed over the top of the hat down onto her chest. Thank goodness his coat was keeping her a little dry. He didn't want her to get sick the first few days she was with him.

Mason had to ride his horse slowly because of the wind and rain. His horse splashed through the water and sloshed through heavy mud. The swaying of the horse's movement caused Abby to drop off to sleep. He pulled her closer into his arms and pushed her head back onto his chest. She certainly was a small creature, and he loved the feel of her warm body snuggled up against his.

The rain felt like small rocks hitting his face and arms, but he told himself that they would be home soon. He glanced under the hat and saw that she slept with her mouth open. He smiled. That didn't surprise him because she seemed like a little magpie that could stand her ground.

Finally, he rode his horse into the barn. The two

young men, Joey and Buster, who worked for him, raced from the bunkhouse to lend him a helping hand. Leaping to the ground, he handed the reins to Joey, the younger of the two men. He reached for Abby and said that introductions would come later. He needed to get her inside the warm house.

"Yes sir, Mr. Mason," the younger boy called back as he led the big bay horse into a stall. The other ranch hand was rooted to the spot with his mouth open. Mason glanced at him and smiled. The man had probably never seen such a pretty gal before.

Mason hurried as fast as his long legs would take him across the yard, onto his porch and into his spacious, warm kitchen. He stood Abby onto her feet and helped remove the soaked jacket. "Can you stand alone or do you need my help to get over to the fire?"

"I'm fine, thank you," she said as she glanced around the large kitchen. Her wide eyes took in the whole place. She seemed overwhelmed, and he thought he heard her say," God help me."

Mason stood in front of the fireplace shifting his body back and forth to the fire. Abby was dripping water on the floor. She didn't seem to be able to move toward the fireplace on her own.   Where was the determined, strong-willed girl who got on his horse and refused his help? She was acting like a scared rabbit.

"Miss Mills, you must move closer to the fire and get warm. I know you're cold because my behind is about frozen. Do you need help?"

"No." She shook her head. "I don't know what to do."

"First, you must get warm. There's a pot of coffee and I will have it warm in just a second." He headed to the big stove, placed a piece of wood down in the burner and moved the coffeepot over the flame.

He returned to the fireplace and removed his wet shirt. Tossing it over the back of a chair, he unbuttoned his white undershirt. Taking a towel off the peg hanging on the wall, he began rubbing his chest and arms until a warm glow covered his firm body.

***

Abby found herself breathless. She had never seen a grown man with his shirt off. She watched his bare chest heave in and out as he grabbed a dry long-sleeve shirt and pulled it over his head without unbuttoning it. He didn't tuck it into his pants but allowed it to flow over his wet trousers.

He glanced at her as he ambled to the stove and poured two cups of hot coffee for them. "Miss Mills, get over here now. We are strangers and I know that you're a little uneasy being in this house with me. You don't have to be so skittish around me. I'm not one of your customers who's going to jump on your lovely body." His wince showed he regretted his words.

"What?" She sucked her breath in, not believing what the stranger had just implied about her. "What did you say?" She wanted him to repeat his remark to her.

She stopped and glared at him. Her body heated up quickly from the fury that flowed through her veins.

He didn't make eye contact with her after his remark. What had he meant? "I asked you a question, sir." Her face reddened and she bore holes in the back of his head.

"Never mind what I said. You need to take your carpetbag and follow me. Since you aren't going to dry in front of the kitchen fireplace, I will light the fire in the guest room." When she didn't comment, he led her down the hall into a lovely bedroom with a small bed. He reached into a bucket that sat by the fireplace and selected a long piece of kindling, struck a match to it and tossed it into the prepared fireplace.

Abby stood silent and stiff as she waited at the doorway for Mason to exit the room. "The water closet is down the hall. It's private so you don't have to worry . . . ." He stopped mid-sentence and said that he would see her in the morning.

***

The scared little girl had reappeared as an angry woman. He heard the big bucket that held the kindle slam into the back of the bedroom door.

Mason hardly slept a wink all night. Down the hall lay the most beautiful girl he had ever set eyes on and she was to be his bride. He had prayed that his uncle would choose a nice young lady, but never in his wildest dreams did he expect Abby Mills. He couldn't believe his blunder last night referring to her customers. How was he ever going to make her believe that he wanted her to have a fresh start? If God had forgiven her, then surely he could, too. He wasn't her judge, only her new bridegroom-to-be.

## Chapter 8

Before daylight, the old rooster announced the beginning of a bright, sunny morning. Mason headed in his bare feet to the kitchen and spoke to Billy, who cooked for him and the other ranch hands. Mason enjoyed the old man's biscuits and fresh coffee every morning. Each night, the men came into the house and they shared supper together in his spacious dining room. But, he had already told the men that they would be taking their evening meal without him in the bunkhouse after his new bride arrived.

"When will I get to meet your new missy? I heard she's a looker."

"Why Billy, you make her sound like one of my prize horses."

"You know I didn't mean no such thing. Just been

waiting, same as you, for your new bride to arrive," Billy said, as he placed a rectangle pan of biscuits in the oven. He wiped his hands on his white apron and asked again. "Well, is she here or still at the wagon train?"

"No, she's in the room down the hall. She's a city gal so I expect she'll soon have to get used to rising early once she's settled in." He turned to go get his boots. "I'm going to look around outside and see what damage the storm did last night," he said as he picked up his coffee cup.

Joey, the young ranch hand, intercepted him as he headed to the barn. "Mr. Mason, you know I put up your horse last night. I rubbed him down and gave him oats." Mason continued to the barn as Joey hurried to keep up with Mason's long strides. "Well, sir, your horse, he's gone! He's not in his stall or the corral. Gone, I can't find him anywhere."

Mason stood perfectly still as the young boy threw his hands up in the air and paced in front of him. "I done woke up all the men and questioned them about the animal. Nobody has seen him."

Mason whirled around, marched into the house and headed straight for Abby's room. Billy watched Mason storm past the breakfast table. He looked over at Joey as he stood in the doorway of the kitchen.

In a flash, Mason was back. "She's gone!" he roared. "Saddle me up a horse now. I'll be right out." Joey ran out of the kitchen with the door slamming behind him.

"What in the world happened to make that gal run

away the first night?" he asked, waving a long fork in the air. "Did you hurt that pretty piece of calico before she got to know you?"

Mason didn't reply to his cook. He stared at him as he took a piece of ham and slammed it between a cut biscuit. "I'll be back soon," he said, as he grabbed a dishrag and covered the sandwich.

Joey was holding a brown horse and tossed the reins to Mason as he jumped on the horse's back. He traveled first to the wagon train. Zeke and Cookie were warming their backsides by the bonfire. The men seemed surprised to see Mason so early.

"Zeke, have you seen Miss Mills this morning on my horse? Sometime during the early morning, she saddled my horse and left the ranch."

"My goodness, little sweet Abby left in the dark on a horse?" He said rubbing his jaw. "That little girl is afraid of the dark and she don't ride horses!"

"So, you didn't hear her pass this way?"

"She done run away from you her first night?" questioned Cookie. "You'd better lay down the law to that gal right off. A good whupping will let her know you're her boss."

"You'd better shut your trap, Cookie, or I'll give you a whupping. Mason ain't going to lay a hand on that sweet child. I'll come with you to look for her," Zeke said, as he pulled his suspenders over his shoulders.

"I'll go alone. I can track her now that it's daylight. I'll let you know when I find her, Zeke." Mason kicked his horse in the sides as he guided him down the trail back toward the Oregon border.

***

Earlier Abby waited until she was sure that Mason was asleep and the rain had stopped before she grabbed her carpetbag and tiptoed out of the house. Careful not to allow the screen door to slam, she scurried across the yard to the big barn. Some of the men were snoring in the bunkhouse.

Mason's bay horse was in his stall. She had never been around a horse unless it was tied to a hitching rail on the street. Abby remembered that men often gave their animal's apples or sugar as a treat, so she had pocketed an apple off the kitchen table so that when she entered the stall she could offer it to the big animal. He was many hands tall and she knew she would never be able to lift a saddle and place it on his back.

Once the horse followed her out of its stall, she gave him the apple. He then decided he would walk out of the barn without her. "Come back, horse," she whispered, but he just kept walking out of the yard, down the path toward the freight wagons. Abby was thankful that Mason didn't have a watchdog. The animal would have awakened the whole place. She was determined to get away from Mason even if she had to walk.

She was thankful the moon was shining bright after the awful rainstorm they had the night before. The moon showed the path. An owl hooted causing her to nearly jump out of her skin. The bottom of her dress was getting wet from the fresh mud holes made in the wide path that led to the ranch house.

Abby didn't care how she looked. She should have put on her trousers, but they were soaking wet. As she struggled to stay on the trail, she couldn't help but think about what Mason had suggested. The nerve of that man suggesting that she had customers. Customers! Oh, where had that come from? She may have lived in a saloon, or brothel to others, but she never had customers.

After walking for several hours, the bright morning sun was a welcome sight because she was afraid of the dark and any wild animals that could be hiding beyond the next tree. Mostly she feared the two-legged creature who would be trailing her now. The sun was hot on her head and face and she had forgotten to put on a sunbonnet. Her face was going to suffer for sure and those awful freckles would be back across her nose. She was hot and thirsty, but she had to keep going before her bridegroom-to-be discovered that she had left.

A big flock of birds flew up from a thicket of tall grass. She stopped walking and listened. Had something spooked them? She felt her body shaking, clouding her thoughts.

Lifting her head to listen to the sounds around her, she heard total silence. Someone was coming, she thought to herself. Slowly she crept as quietly as she could to a large redwood tree and stooped behind it.

Lowering her frame toward the tree, she sunk to the ground.

A branch cracked behind her and she knew without a doubt someone was near. Straining to listen, she didn't hear the clop-clop of a horse. Her body jerked when suddenly a voice directly behind her spoke a warning.

"I hope you're going to come quietly because if you don't, I may have to give you a whupping like one of the men suggested."

Abby leaped to her feet and tried to dodge around the side of the tree away from the giant who was as close as an arm's length away from her.

"You wouldn't dare! Your uncle told me that you wouldn't harm a hair on my head. He said that you were a good man and would protect me with your life."

"Uncle Jackson always speaks the truth, but you are trying my patience, my dear."

"I don't intend to go back with you. You have a very low opinion of me and you think that I'm not fit to be here."

Mason untied his canteen from his saddle and handed it to her. "Drink," he said, with a calm expression.

She wiped her mouth on her sleeve and then she handed him back the water. He offered her a ham sandwich, which she gladly took from him. "Thank you. I didn't realize how thirsty or hungry I was," she said as she glanced up at him and blushed. Memories of his tan muscular chest as he stood in front of the fireplace last night came back to her.

"I know we need to talk about where my uncle met you."

"Your uncle told me that he was writing you all about me. Did you not get his letter?"

"Actually, I didn't. The village has not received mail in quite a while. Our young messenger got hurt and his horse left him stranded. I didn't even know the freight train was here until some young cowpokes came riding into the village yesterday. I came as soon as I heard that it had arrived. The men saw you, too. One of them seemed to know where you lived in San Francisco and about your mama passing away. I'm sorry about that."

"What else did those men say about me?" She asked, determined to know what rumors had been spread about her.

Mason stood looking off into the thick underbrush. He seemed to be choosing his words.

Abby wanted to die on the spot. Strangers were judging her because they knew her mama. Mr. Jackson Waters' nephew believed the terrible gossip about her. Well, the joke was on him because she had traveled miles to get away from San Francisco and the only home she knew. There wasn't any way that she could escape and if she did, where would she go? The saloon was out of the question. "No matter what they're saying about me, Mr. Waters, I guess I am here to stay. I'm the answer to your ad for a mail-order-bride."

## Chapter 9

Mason and his escapee rode back to the wagon train camp. A worried-looking Zeke stood with his foot on a log watching as Mason helped his bride-to-be down off a brown quarter horse. Zeke spit a big wad of used chewing tobacco onto the ground.

Abby hurried to the freight wagon that held the tent she had used while traveling. She crawled inside to gather the last of her things into a larger carpetbag.

While Mason stood next to the fire, he told Zeke that they were going to the Eagle's Station Trading Post and have the preacher marry them.

"Is the gal agreeing to marry up with you?" he said, his face registering concern. "She must have had a good reason for taking off like that in the middle of the night and on foot."

"Don't you be worrying your old-ornery self about my bride. I'll take good care of her, and in time, she'll settle in and be happy."

"Well, all the same to you, I'll be going to the preacher with you. Your uncle put me in charge of her well-being and I'm going to be sure she is okay."

"Fine," Mason said with a shy grin. "Anyway, I need someone to stand up with me." Abby came out of the tent on top of the wagon, and Mason hurried over to help her down. She handed him her belongings but climbed down by herself.

Mason climbed on his horse and pulled Abby up behind him. It didn't take but fifteen minutes to arrive back at the village. Mason stopped on top of a hillside, turned and looked at her. "This is our village. There's the trading post, and the other building is the livery and smithy. Not a lot going on here now, but there's a lot of activity on Saturday." An expression of wonder overtook Abby's face as he motioned for Zeke to follow him.

Mason stopped in front of the store and looped his reins over the hitching rail. "Wait here," he commanded. "I'll only be a minute."

After making arrangements with Mr. Peterson and the preacher, he exited the store and again offered to help Abby down off the horse, and this time she accepted. Zeke jumped off his mule, wrapped his reins around the hitching post and all three entered the building.

***

As they climbed the steps to a dimly-lit room, Abby froze. Standing near the back of the room was a tall, bearded man holding a book, a Bible, she was sure. All the days of her newly acclaimed freedom were fading away. Zeke took her arm and as she placed one foot in front of the other, they made their way to the man. As if in a daze, she heard the man speak.

"I see you didn't take the time to dress in your finery. I suppose you're in a big hurry too, just like your man," he chuckled at his own private joke.

Abby glanced down at herself and smoothed her hair. She was a mess after sneaking out of the house in the middle of the night and trudging over the muddy trail. The thought that today would be her wedding day never crossed her mind.

This was not the way she had dreamed her wedding day would be. She peered down at her muddy blue calico dress and wanted to cry. Tears were held in check behind her eyelids, but she knew any minute they would spill onto her cheeks. She looked at Mason, but before she could speak, Mrs. Peterson, the shopkeeper's wife, descended the stairs. She took one glance at Abby and immediately took both of her hands into hers.

"My goodness, gentlemen, this pretty little lady needs to freshen up before she's married. Come, child. I'll help you. My name is Marie Peterson. Do you have something else to wear?"

Abby glanced at Mason and he hurried out the door and retrieved her carpetbag. Mrs. Peterson shouldered the bag, took Abby by the elbow and led her from the room. "We won't be long," she said in a sing-song voice.

Marie Peterson must have seen the terrified look on the young girl's face when she came down the stairs. "Now, child, I'm not your mama, but I want to know if you are wanting to marry up with that Waters' boy. He's nice enough, that's for sure, but no one can force another person to do something like marrying another if they don't want."

"I made a deal with his uncle that I would travel here and marry him. In return, his nephew would care for me and give me a home. Even if I felt different about marrying him, the deed is done. I am here and I'm going to honor my promise," Abby said, fighting back tears.

"Well then, let's get you in some clean clothes and put some color back in those lovely cheeks of yours. The menfolk are waiting. "

An hour later, stiff and unsmiling, Abby inched down the stairs and stood at the bottom step. Mason had taken the opportunity to clean himself up. His hair was combed and he wore a new plaid shirt. Mason smiled as he greeted her with a slight bow. He lifted her palm to his lips and a slight whiff of vanilla greeted his nose.

Abby smoothed the green and white calico dress and straightened the lovely white ribbon holding her long golden hair back from her face. When it was time to take her place, she moved mechanically. She took one step, then Zeke pulled her toward the front, step by step. She peered around at the walls in the old building, but saw nothing. There was no Mama, no friends, no music, and no flowers. She didn't have a lovely white gown with all the finery that went with it. This was supposed to be a wonderful day filled with happiness, but it wasn't.

A loud voice brought her back to reality. She stood in an old store that smelled of coffee beans and gun oil. Zeke had stopped walking. She was standing next to the tall, powerful stranger who was going to have control over her for as long as they both lived. She trembled. Why had she agreed to come here and marry a man whom she had never met? Mr. Waters assured her that she would be safe and his nephew was a good man. A good man all right, one who believed he was being forced to marry a woman with loose morals.

Her body shook so hard that Mason asked if she was cold. She refused to meet his eyes, but moved her head right to left.

The preacher cleared his throat and gestured for Zeke and Marie to take their places next to the bride and groom. "Let's get this marriage said and done."

Time seemed to stand still as the preacher drummed the words from his mouth. Every nerve in Abby's body screamed. She heard Mason repeat the words that the preacher said.

"I, Mason Jackson Waters, take you Abby Mills to be my lawful wedded wife—"

In just above a whisper—she was happy that she didn't stumble over the same words, she made her vow, pledging herself to this stranger. In the next moment, he was sliding a gold band on her finger, and then they bowed their heads for a closing prayer.

"I believe it is customary for a groom to kiss his bride," the preacher said as he grinned at everyone.

Mason gazed into his bride's eyes, leaned down, and quickly kissed her lips. Her first kiss.

"Congratulations, my boy," Zeke said, as he regained Mason's attention away from his new bride. "There's plenty of time for those shenanigans. We've a freight train to unload. The boys are wanting to get on back to San Francisco."

"Sure. Just give me a minute." Mason took Abby by the arm and approached the preacher. He thanked the man and gave him some money for his trouble.

"Peterson, I am taking Abby back to the ranch and I will be back soon to help unload the supplies that my uncle sent to you." Mason held Abby's hand and led her outside. He tossed her up on his horse and climbed up behind her like he had done before.

"Surely, I can ride your horse back to the ranch without your help," she said.

"Have you ever ridden a horse?" When Abby didn't answer, Mason gave a small grunt. "We'll give you some lessons soon enough."

After Mason left her alone at the ranch house, she was free to look around. It was a grand place for sure and it was to be hers—and his. She yawned while checking out the parlor with its lovely, tall windows covered with yards of white muslin material.

"This will never do," she said to herself as she realized how tired she was. She gazed out the window at the lovely landscape. This was her home and she was married to a handsome young man. She pulled on the white material that covered the windows and sighed. It had only been six weeks since she left her grief behind and now she was feeling shame. Shame because she had lived in a saloon and her mother had been considered a bad woman. Now her husband wasn't sure if she wasn't just like her mama. Was she 'tainted' too because she lived in the saloon?

Shaking her head, Abby made her way back to the guest room that she used the night before and slipped off her soft slippers. For now, she would pray that God would give her the courage, which she desperately needed to meet each day as it came. Stretching out on the bed, she fell asleep.

It seemed like only minutes had passed but the sound of someone walking around in the house woke her up. It was still daylight outside.

She was still wearing her green calico dress. Smoothing her skirt, she plodded toward the dresser and used her fingers to comb her hair back and retied the golden curls with the white ribbon. After she felt presentable, she headed to the kitchen, but stopped in the doorway.

Mason was standing at the stove with his hand on the cold coffeepot. He spun around to face her.

The two strangers' eyes met for the first time since they'd spoken their wedding vows. Abby inched into the kitchen. "Please, let me make some coffee. I guess I was really tired because I slept most of the day away. Would you like some supper? I am a good cook, so people say." She stopped talking and waited for him to say something.

"Coffee will be fine and a couple of cold sandwiches will do for tonight. You need to rest some more and I'm exhausted from unloading the wagons. The old man, Zeke, will be heading back to San Francisco tomorrow. He would like to see you before he pulls out."

Mason waited for her reply.

Abby only smiled.

"I think he would be happy to take you back with him, if that's what you want to do," Mason said.

Abby's eyes widened at his offer to go home with Zeke. It had only been this morning that they united as husband and wife. Was he so displeased with her that he wanted her to leave? He did believe that she was a soiled dove and wasn't fit to be his wife. Tears filled her eyes from embarrassment as she turned her face away from his view.

"Are you saying that you want me to leave?" Abby held her breath and prayed that he would give her a chance.

"That's not what I said." He was quiet for a moment and then asked, "Do you want to go back with him?"

Abby stood silent for a moment. Was he so disgusted with her that he wanted her to get on the wagon train and hightail it back to San Francisco? "I will leave . . . if . . . you want me to go." She avoided his eyes and bowed her head.

"Well, woman, are you going to stand there all night or are you going to feed your new husband?"

His words didn't register at first but when she peered up at him, she caught a glimpse of a smile. Abby took a deep breath. Hurrying by him, she charged to the sink and pumped a big pot of water. After placing ground coffee beans into it, she placed it over the hot flame. She guessed this was his answer to her reply. She was staying for better or worse.

## Chapter 10

As they ate the light supper, Mason told her that he had purchased different pieces of furniture for the house. "The furniture is stored out in the barn. You can ask a couple of the men to help you bring in a piece or two. Once you decide where you want them placed, they can bring in more. This is your home now and I want you to arrange the furniture to your satisfaction. There are several pieces that I had chosen to go into my office."

"Mr. Waters, surely you'll want to put the furniture where you want it."

"My name is Mason." He glared at her. "I just said that this is your new home now. I brought the furniture to please my new bride."

"Of course." Abby glanced at him and said, "I would like to make some drapes for the parlor. That muslin material can be used for many things, but not window dressing."

"So, you can sew?" He appeared surprised that she had already noticed the ugly white muslin material being used for drapes.

"One of the requirements for your mail-order bride was that she was able to sew, I believe." She kept her eyes fastened on her folded hands in her lap.

"Yes, I believe that's true," he said with a discernable wince, "but, I can afford to order anything you want."

"How can it be my home if I don't put my heart and soul into caring for it?"

Mason lifted his eyebrows and smiled. "You've made a good point."

Mason glanced around at the kitchen. He stretched and yawned. "Pardon me, but I think it's time for us to retire. You can sleep in because Billy will cook breakfast."

"This Billy fellow, does he cook all your meals?"

"Yep, he has since I hired him to cook for my ranch hands."

"As your wife, I want to prepare the meals. I can cook, and besides, what will I do with my time if I don't cook, clean and sew?" She tilted her head to meet his eyes, waiting for an answer. .

***

Mason was shocked that his lovely bride wanted to get up before sunrise and cook for him, maybe pack a lunch and prepare a big hearty meal for dinner. Billy cooked beans, potatoes, burnt steaks and more beans for each meal. Mason had hit another gold mine with this girl's household talents and willingness to work.

"Breakfast is at five each morning. Do you think you will be ready to start each day that early?" He really didn't know anything about his new bride's past.

"Watch me," she said as she cleared his plate and coffee cup from the table. He headed to his room carrying a tea kettle of hot water.

"Goodnight," she said.

Mason stopped and looked at her as she washed and dried the few dishes. Oh no, my sweet, he thought. It is not goodnight—yet.

***

Abby placed the few dishes in the cabinet over the counter, checked the back door to make sure it was locked, and blew out the lantern that sat in the middle of the big wooden table that could seat at least eight grown men.

As she made her way to her room, Mason called to her. "Abby, that's the guest room. You aren't a guest any longer. This is your room now."

Abby whirled around and peered into his room. A lovely quilt covered a small double-sized bed. A large dresser with many drawers was placed on one wall and a tall wardrobe was positioned on the other side. A big rocker sat in front of the stone fireplace with a woven rug lying in front of it. This was a lovely room, fit for a king, except for the small bed, but she wasn't ready to be the queen.

"Mason, I thank you for the offer, but this is your room. Where will you sleep if I take this room?"

"Mrs. Waters, this is our room. We will share this room."

"Surely you don't expect me to sleep with you after only meeting you two days ago. Your uncle said that he would ask you to give me—us—time to get to know each other before… before…you know…"

"Are you saying that he wrote this in his letter, the letter that I have not received?"

"Yes. Mrs. Roberta and your uncle discussed this before I agreed to come here." *Please, don't let this man, this stranger, make me consummate our marriage so soon*, she prayed silently.

Mason slammed out of the room and out into the darkness of the night. Abby sighed. Thank goodness, she thought. Maybe she won that round.

She went into the guest room and retrieved her white muslin gown that wasn't as warm as the flannel gown she had packed. She unbraided her golden blonde hair and brushed it with quick strokes, then used the water in the basin that Mason had left untouched and washed her face and rinsed her mouth with some soda water. Hurrying she pulled back the lovely quilt and slid under it and snuggled. This was heaven, she thought.

Before she got comfortable, Mason entered the room. He looked down at her and stated in no uncertain terms, "We may not live as man and wife for a while, at least until we get to know each other better, but this is my bed and I am sleeping in it."

Abby scooted out from under the quilt. She wished she had remembered to bring her robe into this room. "Certainly, I will go back to the other room."

"No! We'll share this bed together. You're my wife and you will sleep with me." He glared at her with daggers in his eyes. "There's a bigger bed in the barn with all of the other furniture that I ordered. So choose your side for now and climb right back under those covers."

Abby had never slept with anyone before. Once in a while, Lucinda would allow her to climb in bed with her if it was storming. But, to sleep with a man—what would her mama think of her?

Mason stared at Abby's pale face. "Don't tell me you're afraid. That would be a joke."

Abby sucked in her breath and quickly jerked back the covers. She retrieved several large pillows from the closet and placed them down the middle of the bed. "Since we don't have a bundling board, these pillows will have to act as one. You stay on your side of the bed, and I'll stay on mine." She climbed in the bed, turned on her side and lay near the edge of the mattress with the quilt pulled up to her chin. "The fool thinks I have slept with every man in San Francisco," she murmured to herself.

"Careful you don't roll off the bed," he said with a

sarcastic laugh.

***

Mason wanted to pull his new wife into his arms. He had waited two years for this lovely creature. To be honest, he never believed that his uncle would find someone as unique as this girl. He wanted to hold her and share his dreams of the future he had planned for them. But for now, restraint and patience were required. If she had worked in a saloon and entertained men, she would have desire for him soon. He tugged on the covers, trying hard to get comfortable with a large pillow in his back and not much room on his side of the bed.

***

During the night, the pillows had been pushed to the bottom of the bed. Mason's body heat acted like a magnet to Abby. She found herself snuggled up against his back. Several times she woke to find her head placed on his shoulder or her legs tossed across his. She couldn't believe that she could be so relaxed with him in her sleep.

They'd gone to bed earlier than normal because it had been such a busy day. They even got married early, after he'd stayed up most of the night chasing after her. Then he'd worked hard all day unloading the freight wagons. She could tell he was awake. Sighing, she rolled over to face him as he turned to look into her eyes.

"Good morning, sweet. Did you sleep well? I hope I wasn't a bed hog," he said smiling at her.

Sweet. He called her sweet. She liked that. Maybe just maybe he wasn't sure about her, she thought as she looked into his eyes. He reached toward her and traced his finger down the side of her face, placing a strand of hair behind her ear. Could he hear her heart pounding? Leaning his face toward her, she felt his breath as his lips attempted to cover hers. Without any thought, she quickly scooted away from him and tumbled onto the floor.

Mason jumped out of bed rushing around to her side of the bed.

Abby lay tangled in the sheet and twisted quilt. When he saw her, he gave a soft laugh at her predicament. He reached for her, and another chuckle emerged from his mouth. Before he knew it, he couldn't control himself. He sat down on the bed and laughed until his sides ached.

Abby attempted to rise, but Mason's laughter was contagious. Both of them laughed until they couldn't laugh anymore.

He reached for her hand, and as she touched his, she felt herself blushing from her head to her toes. Abby was holding onto the covers as she stood and continued to hold part of the quilt in front of her body. She couldn't take her eyes away from Mason as he stood, straight and tall in his white knee-length underwear. She lowered her eyes and smiled.

He must have realized his state of undress and quickly bowed and rushed to the water closet. Now that she had a chance to escape, she ran to the guest room and put on her white robe. Marching as fast as possible, she raced to the kitchen and placed a pot of coffee on the stove. Making sure it was getting hot, she hurried to the guest room to dress. As she pulled her lovely dresses out of the large carpetbag, she noticed they were rumpled and would need to be pressed before wearing. She reached in her smaller bag and retrieved a pair of her pants and a plaid long-sleeved shirt.

When she returned to the kitchen, Mason gave her a disapproving glance as he drank a cup of coffee. "Coffee is good. Thank you."

***

"I will have some bacon and flapjacks in few minutes."

As promised, she placed a stack of fluffy flapjacks with a small tray of crispy bacon in front of him. A large jar of dark, thick syrup and a bowl of butter joined them.

She slid into a chair next to him and sipped a small cup of coffee that was more milk than coffee. "Where is your plate?" he asked concerned that she wasn't going to join him at mealtime. This was one thing he had missed since leaving his uncle's home. He enjoyed sharing a meal with family and having conversations.

"I will eat something later, if you don't mind. I'm not used to eating this early. It's only five o'clock in the morning," she replied with a shy smile.

"Sorry, I forgot that you're a city gal, but ranch life starts early here. You'll soon get used to it." He placed his napkin beside his plate, stood and pushed his chair back under the table. "The men will be having their noon meal with us. Please prepare plenty to eat."

As he placed his Stetson on his head, he turned to her and said, "Dress a little more appropriate, like the 'lady' you are."

***

Abby's face paled at his last remark. "Dress like the lady I am?" What did he mean by that? Abby watched him walk to the barn. After the night they shared together, he still believed that she was one of the "ladies" that worked upstairs at The Red Dog Saloon. How was she going to convince him she was a good woman, not a tainted girl? The longer she sat at the table, the more embarrassed and angrier she became. "Dress like the 'lady' that he thinks I am! Yes, I will do just that," she said aloud to herself, smiling.

# Chapter 11

bby wanted to please the ranch hands who worked for Mason by preparing them a nice hot lunch. She went down in the cellar, dug into the pork barrel, and selected a large pork roast. Surveying the room, she discovered sweet potatoes and several jars of green beans. After preparing the roast for the oven, she washed and cleaned the potatoes. Lucinda taught her to bake the big orange sweet potatoes in the stove, skin and all. She placed the green beans in a big pot, covered them with water and poured bacon grease into them. She would bake biscuits and corn bread to serve with the meal. Looking further in the pantry, she found a big basket of green apples. Pies being her specialty, she prepared the crust and made three large apple pies.

Lunch would be ready when the men arrived so it

was time to 'ready herself.' She didn't want to disappoint Mason.

As Abby applied her mama's paint to her lovely innocent face, she was disappointed that Mason was so disillusioned about her. Why did he choose to believe the worst about her? If only he had received his uncle's letter of introduction, he would have known the truth. Well, she thought as she applied more eye make-up over her lovely green eyes, if he wanted her to look like the "lady" that he thought her to be, so be it. She wanted to please him.

****

Mason stepped on the back porch and peeked into the kitchen. The aroma of the pork roast and fresh apple pies made his stomach growl. He stepped out the door and rang the dinner bell. It wasn't but a few minutes before the men appeared in the kitchen. They looked to Mason and he motioned for them to take a seat. As he walked over to the stove to get the coffeepot, he heard chairs slide back and the rustle of boots as the men stood. He looked toward the door of the kitchen and froze. There standing just inside the warm room was Abby . . . his Abby?

"Good afternoon. Please take your seats while I begin by helping Mason get your coffee."

Mason turned to his men. All six of them were staring at her like she was a sea monster. Their eyes were bulging and their mouths were wide open.

"Out!" Mason yelled as he pivoted toward them. Chairs went flying backwards and boots stomped out the door. The men glanced back over their shoulders and hurried outside.

Mason slowly circled to face Abby. "What do you think you're doing with all that face paint smeared from here to there?" He yelled as the veins in his neck enlarged and his hands clenched into tight fists.

"Whatever do you mean, Mason?" She asked in a sweet, soft tone. "You said for me to dress appropriately. Like the *lady* you seem to think I am." She swayed her hips just out of his reach. "Don't you like the way I look?"

"No. Go clean that mess off your face and fix your dress," he demanded, glancing down at her chest. All he could see was a lovely locket dangling from her neck to the center of her bosom.

"Why? I think I look just like you think I should look."

Before she knew what had happened, Mason took a giant step, grabbed her hand and jerked her small frame over to the sink. He took a clean rag from under the counter and dipped it into a pail of water, then wiped it across her mouth, removing the bright red paint that she had used on her lovely soft lips. He wiped her rosy cheeks and tilted her head back until she thought he might break her neck. Once he was satisfied that he had scrubbed the majority of the paint from her face, he gazed down into her lovely face.

Even with paint smeared across her lips they were irresistible. He captured the back of her head with his hand and lowered his lips over hers, kissing her hard. The lovely rose scent in her hair almost made him lose complete control. He wanted to ravish her right there on the kitchen floor. In a split second, he pulled himself back together, not understanding how he could have lost control of himself.

He pulled her body closer and began trying to close the top button on her dress front. Flustered with the buttons, he tossed her across his shoulder giving her backside a hard slap as she screamed for him to put her down. He strode to their bedroom and dropped her in the middle of the bed.

"I'll serve the men their lunch and you best be the lady that I married when I return this evening."

Abby sat up in the middle of the bed on her knees. "I didn't think that you believed I was a decent girl. I was just being the 'lady' that you thought me to be!" She screamed and rolled off the bed away from him.

"We'll talk tonight—about what or who you are. Let me get out of here before I do something we both may regret." Mason spun around and slammed the bedroom door. He could hear her laughter from the other side of the door.

Mason called the men back inside and they served each other the noon meal. It was the best food that Mason or any of his men had ever eaten. Everything was cooked to perfection, seasoned just right, and delicious. The men practically inhaled the apple pies.

"Mr. Mason," said Joey, "well, sir, I don't rightly know why your pretty wife was dressed like that, but I've seen her before. She's beautiful, and well golly, she shore can cook." He looked around the table at the other men who were all nodding and smiling. "Please don't send her away. I would sure hate to have to go back to Billy's cooking."

"Sorry, you all had to witness our little disagreement just a few minutes ago, but all is better now. I can assure you." He prayed he was telling them the truth, "Abby is here to stay."

***

After washing her face and dressing in a blue calico housedress and soft blue slippers, Abby heated the iron in the kitchen, pressed her dresses and hung them in the wardrobe. She unpacked both carpetbags and placed her clothes in the dresser and her mama's items in the bottom drawer. She returned to the kitchen and washed and put away all the items that she used to make lunch. There was only part of one apple pie left, which told her that the men loved sweets.

Placing a big pot of pinto beans on the stove to simmer all afternoon, she would make a hot and spicy chili and serve it with rice and squares of hot cornbread. Abby decided to make several large pans of cinnamon rolls and pour a white creamy sauce over them for dessert. She walked out to the spring house to make sure there was extra milk being chilled so she could serve some with the rolls.

As she passed the barn, Abby entered and saw furniture pieces stacked on top of each other and more covered with white sheets. She peeked under the covers and was amazed how lovely some of the pieces were. Mason said that this was to be her job to bring in the furniture and place the pieces where she would like them to go.

Hurrying back inside the kitchen, she checked her beans and sliced the beef roast into small pieces. She added them to the beans with her hot spices and covered the lid. In several hours, she would bake the bread and dinner would be ready.

Surveying the parlor and the two lovely guest rooms, she selected pieces of furniture that would be perfect for each room. As she returned to the barn, she found Joey rubbing down one of the spare horses.

"Hello, Joey," Abby said. "Mr. Waters said I could ask you or some other ranch hand to help me with some of this furniture." She gestured toward the big stack of covered items.

"Yes, madam, be glad to help you. Have you picked something out for me to carry to the house for you?"

The rest of the afternoon, Joey and Abby busied themselves with placing new items here and there. Joey was patient whenever Abby changed her mind and had him carry the piece back outside and then have him go get it again. They stopped, had lemonade, and talked about family.

Joey was the same age as Abby, but she'd thought he was much older. He told her that he had been on his own since he was twelve. His step-father was mean and tried to work him to death, so the first chance he got, he left. She thought of her childhood. At least she had a mama who loved her, although she had no other family members or friends.

Now, as she worked beside Joey, she thought, maybe at last she had a new friend.

Mason came in earlier than normal and discovered Joey and Abby in the bedroom as they discussed the placement of a table under the window. They both held the table, moving it a few inches back and forth and laughed as they tried to decide where it should be positioned.

"You say where to place it," laughed Joey. "It's your table, after all."

"I'll make the decision," Mason said, with a rough tone of voice as his eyes darted from Joey to Abby. "Place it there where you have it."

Joey blushed and said that he'd better get back to the barn. Abby trailed after him and called a thank you to his back as he scooted across the yard to the barn.

"Well, I hope you're satisfied. You just embarrassed that young man who has been helping me all afternoon. You should be grateful that you have such a nice ranch hand who is well-mannered and thoughtful," Abby said as she attempted to circle around Mason.

"Of course, you're right. I didn't mean to be so rough on him. I'll talk with him later before supper," he said, as he looked at the new added pieces of furniture.

"This place is shaping into a home with the new furnishings. I see you have been working hard and I can smell supper. The men loved your noon meal, by the way. They asked me not to send you away." He smiled down at her as she stood next to the bedroom door.

"Were you thinking about sending me back?"

"No, but another stunt like you pulled this morning might cause me to do something that we both won't like." He grinned as he took her arm. "Let's go into the kitchen and finish getting supper ready."

Mason sat at his desk in the corner of the kitchen while sneaking glances at Abby as she whipped up the cornbread and placed it in the oven. She uncovered the cinnamon rolls and prepared them to go into the oven when she took out the bread. She set the table with the silverware and napkins and placed large bowls for the chili on the work counter. The rice was in a large ceramic-covered bowl sitting next to them.

"Abby, if you ever feel that you need help in the house or with the cooking, please feel free to tell me. I can afford to get you someone to come and help. Helen comes every Monday to do the wash, and I would like to continue that. She needs the money."

"I will need help when I start canning and putting up preserves. I helped in our kitchen when Lucinda put up a few things. I enjoyed making jams and jellies."

"That's nice to hear. My mama used to put up vegetables. I helped her in the small garden." It was nice to have a normal conversation with his bride.

"Mr. Waters told me about your parents. I'm sorry." Abby said.

"Is the meal about ready? I'll go tell the men to wash up. They have worked hard today getting ready for our new horses."

Abby took out the pans of cornbread and put in the cinnamon rolls to bake. In just a few minutes, the room smelled wonderful. The men filed in with their heads hanging down and their eyes averted.

***

Abby waited until all the men were in the room. She could feel a blush coming over her body from embarrassment. She smiled at them, cleared her throat and softly began to speak.

"I want to apologize for the way I acted at the noon meal. I'm sorry you had to witness that from me. Please forgive me."

The men fell all over themselves with big grins and little hand gestures. "It's all right, don't fret none. We've seen worse," were a few of the comments coming from across the room. Abby smiled and filled their bowls with the spicy chili and rice. The cornbread and butter were already on the table along with the syrup. Abby glanced at Mason and smiled. She felt that he had forgiven her, too.

After the men devoured the cinnamon rolls and cold milk, they left the kitchen to ready themselves for bed. Mason had said morning came early on the ranch.

Abby begin to remove the dirty dishes from the table when Mason joined her. He stacked the bowls, cups and saucers beside the washtub that was used for washing the dishes. "Thank you, Mason, but you don't have to help me. I know you must be tired, too."

"I am tired, but you have done your share of hard work today. I am beginning to feel bad that I haven't hired a lady to come in to take care of these things." He said, pointing at the dishes.

"I said earlier that I would let you know when I need help. Please go do whatever you do after supper and let me get busy here. It won't take me long, and then maybe you and I can talk about why and how I came to be here."

"Yes, we do need to get a few things cleared up between us."

Abby's chin quivered as she turned her head away from him. Tears sprang to her eyes when she thought of her mama and her plans for her to leave the only home she had ever known. Mama wanted her to be safe and get away from San Francisco. Well, I am certainly a long ways from The Red Dog Saloon, she thought.

***

Mason started to walk over to her but decided against it. Once they had their talk, maybe he would understand what the tears were all about. "I'll go check on the sow that is about to have a litter. Joey and Buster are supposed to be watching out for her, but I want to see for myself how she's coming along."

# Chapter 12

Mason entered the house and found the kitchen and parlor empty. He figured that Abby had gone to take care of a few personal needs. Pulling the rocker over in front of the low-burning fire, he stoked the wood before sitting down. He watched the fire blaze before adding another small log to it. The house was enormous so each night he built a fire.

Taking his Bible down from the mantel, he opened it and read a scripture that jumped off the page at him. Matthew 26:41: *"Watch and pray so that you will not fall into temptation. The spirit is willing, but the flesh is weak."* He closed the Bible, shut his eyes and prayed. "Oh, Lord, help me, for I know I am weak when it comes to this new bride of mine," he mumbled quietly.

***

After preparing the kitchen for the next day, Abby walked toward the parlor when someone knocked loudly on the back door. As she started toward the door, Mason said that he would answer it.

"Mason, sir," Joey practically yelled. "The sow, she's having a lot of trouble delivering her babies. Buster and I don't know what to do. Can you come and have a look at her?"

"Where's Mick?" Mason asked, wondering why his foreman wasn't outback helping the two young men.

"Don't know, but he ain't around. Can you come?" Joey urged, clearly concerned about his boss's prize sow.

"Give me a minute to slip on my boots. I'll be right behind you." Mason turned to Abby. "Sorry, you go on to bed. I'll be in after I help with the sow. Sure don't want to lose her."

"You sure you don't want me to stay up? I could make you some coffee?"

"Thank you, but you have to get an early start in the morning. We'll talk tomorrow night, but thanks again for the offer." He said and watched her walk down the hall toward their room.

Mason hurried out to the side of the barn to see what was happening to his sow. He had checked on her before going into the parlor to have a talk with Abby. There were signs of milk forming on her teats, which indicated that she would be giving birth within the next twenty-four hours if not sooner.

"This is her first batch of babies and she's nervous," Mason told the two boys. "Watch her closely. I'm going into the bunkhouse."

The bunkhouse was empty. All the ranch hands were gone, but clothes still hung on the pegs and personal items were scattered all around. He walked into the barn and their horses were missing.

"Joey, where are the men?" Mason asked, concerned and a little confused as to why they were not in their bunks asleep or playing a game of cards. Billy, the cook, was snoozing away.

"Well, it ain't for me to rightly say." The young man hung his head and stuffed his hands in his back pockets.

"I asked you a question, and I want an answer now and be quick about it," Mason snapped at the young man. He couldn't imagine where the men had gone.

"My guess is they're probably visiting the shacks that are in the woods near the next village. A few of them go almost every night and some of the others only go once or twice a week." He rubbed a circle in the dirt with his boot, clearly hating to squeal to the boss about the men's nightly activities.

"Let's get back to the sow, and I will take care of the men in the morning. I can't let this sow die. She should have a litter of about ten piglets."

Around three in the morning, the big sow gave birth to nine healthy babies. The delivery was long and hard for the mama sow. The sow's membrane had to be removed several times from the new babies to keep them from suffocating.

Joey washed his hands many times with lye soap and hot water so he could reach into the birthing canal and gently but firmly move a piglet into position. Buster had prepared a warm basket with old quilts and hay to lay the newborn babies in while the others were being born and to keep the mama from lying on them. The mama lay on her side in a batch of clean hay while the boys positioned her babies on her stomach to nurse.

"Good job, boys. I appreciate your help. I'll see that you get a little extra in your pay at the end of the month. Go on to bed. Our mama will be fine the rest of the night," Mason said as he stretched.

Mason washed up at the pump and slipped off his boots at the back door. He walked softly to his bedroom. Spread out in the middle of his big bed lay his new beautiful bride. The pillows used as a bundling board were tossed on his side.

He grinned, thinking that the bundling board idea was ridiculous.

He wanted to lie down, snuggle her into his arms, and devour her lovely rose-scented body, but he knew he couldn't do that. His body had been racked with nerves over his new sow, angry with the ranch hands who had slipped away to have some fun and frustrated to the point that he wanted to ravish his bride with or without her consent. He turned and quietly went into the guest bedroom. He placed his hands on the dresser, peered into the mirror, hung his head and prayed, *Oh, Lord, please help me.*

A decision came over him, and he knew it was the right thing to do before he did harm to her and their relationship. He would not share her bed until she asked him to be her husband. It had been his idea—no—his demand that they sleep together. Thinking that if she was close to him each night, she would want to be his bride, but that had not been the case. It was punishment for him to lie in bed and watch her sleep, and at times to feel her wrapping her arms around his waist while she slept. He was just too weak to be that close to her any longer.

# Chapter 13

After breakfast the next morning, Mason kissed Abby on the forehead as he prepared to go to work. She stepped back from him, but then gave him a sweet smile. He would see her at the noon meal. Mason looked pleased that she didn't act skittish when he kissed her.

"Mason, did you sleep in the barn last night?" Abby had lain awake for hours waiting for him to come to bed. She had drifted off to sleep, but when she awoke, she could tell that he hadn't slept in their bed.

"No, I slept in the guest room and that's where I intend to sleep from now on." He looked down at the floor as he answered her.

"Why the sudden change of beds?" she asked.

"Look, I can sleep where I choose. But to answer your question, I'm afraid that I can't continue to keep my promise to you if I lie beside you night after night. You will have to let me know when you're ready to be my wife, in every way."

He whirled around and stormed out the back door, clearly angry and embarrassed that he had to explain his actions as to where and why he slept somewhere different.

Abby slowly walked behind him to the back screen door and watched as he led his horse out of the barn. She stayed in the shadow of the door and admired the way he checked his horse and riding gear. What had made him change his mind about their sleeping arrangement? The first night she came to the ranch, he had demanded that they sleep in the same bed.

***

He was aware that Abby continued to watch him as he ran his hand under the saddle and smoothed the blanket. Next, he examined the horse's front hoof and ran his hand down the leg of the animal and gave it a good pat. The bit in the animal's mouth needed adjusting so Mason took the reins and fixed it. After he was satisfied that all was well with the horse's equipment, Mason whispered something into his ear that the horse seemed to understand and he shook his head, tossing his long mane in all directions. Mason patted the animal and gave a chuckle while climbing on the big brown bay.

Abby was still watching him, but when he smiled at

her, she jumped back away from the doorway. He was sure she was curious about him and this pleased him. He was certainly fascinated with her, too.

***

Abby began preparing lunch by placing a large pot of dried beans on the stove to cook. She pulled out her flour bowl and prepared several pie crusts. There were only a dozen or so ripe apples left in the pantry bin so she decided to use them. When she returned from the pantry, she froze and searched around in hopes of seeing one of the men nearby. In her kitchen stood an old Indian woman who stared at her like she was a mirage.

"Who are you in my cooking space?" the older woman demanded in broken English.

"I'm Abby Mills, I mean Waters. This is my kitchen. Who are you?" Abby tried not to appear afraid even though her knees felt weak. She had never seen anyone that looked like this little woman. Where were Joey or Buster when she needed them?

"I Cactus Flower. I away, but I back. I cook for Sunday Boy."

"Sunday Boy?" Abby asked with much curiosity. "Who is that?"

Cactus Flower eased over and stood close to Abby. She examined her as if she was a stupid White woman. She reached to touch Abby's hair which had been plaited into a long rope that hung down her back.

Abby never took her eyes away from the small

creature, but when she reached for her hair, Abby jumped away from her, not sure if the old woman was going to harm her. Grabbing the carving knife off the counter that she had been using to cut the pastry crust, Abby took several steps back.

Cactus Flower looked surprised at the petite White girl and immediately pulled out the eighteen-inch blade that she wore on her leg. She grinned at Abby, showing off her big shiny white tooth in the front of her mouth, then screamed a warrior chant and bent her small body into a warrior stance.

Abby screamed and jumped as far away as she could from the small Indian woman. Cactus Flower inched toward Abby as she continued her chant in some foreign language that Abby didn't understand.

Mason entered the back door and froze. There in the kitchen was a standoff between two female warriors. To his amazement, his sweet wife held a small carving knife high in the air with her right hand while Cactus Flower, his Indian housekeeper, waved her long sharp blade in front of her small frame. They were circling the kitchen counter. Mason didn't know if he should get between them or enjoy the situation.

***

"My Lord, Cactus Flower! When did you get home?" Neither warrior answered. Abby was relieved to see Mason, but she was too afraid to move. Cactus Flower straightened up, lowered her weapon and gave

Mason a big grin as she spoke.

"She brave woman. I could cut her into many pieces, but she don't run. She only screamed like most silly White women." She placed her long blade back into the strap on her side.

Abby smiled timidly at Mason, laid the carving knife back on the counter and lowered herself into a chair at the kitchen table. She rested her head on her arms to stave off the spinning room. Never had she been so scared in her life.

"Abby, this little woman is Cactus Flower who has worked for me ever since I moved here." Mason placed his arm around the little woman's shoulders. "She has been away for many weeks to care for family members who live in a village north of here. I forgot to tell you about her."

"Yes, *Sunday Boy*, you did." She glared at him with daggers in her eyes. Never had she dreamed that she would meet a wild Indian who might cut her into many pieces without batting an eye. She couldn't even remember meeting an Indian when she lived in San Francisco.

"Now, Abby, don't you start calling me that name. A few of the Indians and the old men that hang around the trading post call me that because I don't smoke, chew tobacco or partake of their old rotgut, moonshine. I don't want to hear that name at home."

Abby smelled the beans that were boiling and hurried over to the stove, lifted the lid and stirred them.

Cactus Flower peeked over her shoulder and said, "I have a fresh possum lying outside. I will bring it in and you can cook it in the beans."

"No!" Abby yelled. "I'm…. going to make bean soup for the noon meal."

Mason laughed as he witnessed the look on Abby's face. He was doubtful that she had ever eaten any wild critters, much less cooked them.

"Now, Cactus Flower, Abby will be doing most of the cooking now that she's my wife." Cactus Flower raised her eyebrows to question him, but she remained quiet.

"I'm sure she would like to have you help her prepare some of the food, but today, why don't you take your fresh kill on down to Peterson and sell it to him."

Mason started to lead Cactus Flower to the back door. "I be back tomorrow after sun is up in the sky. Not too early. White women sleep morning away."

Abby had recovered from her fright and remembered her manners. This old woman had worked for Mason for several years. Abby didn't want her to feel that she had lost her job because Mason had taken a wife.

"Cactus Flower, please come anytime you wish. Mason and I want you to continue working here just like before. I like to cook, but I could use your help. Feeding six grown men is a lot of work."

Cactus Flower held her head down as she made her way to the back door. She stopped and turned to look at Abby. As quiet as she came in, she left, but not before she said, "Tomorrow. But, sell my possum, rabbits and squirrels to old man Peterson today."

*** 

After several weeks, Abby's and Mason's life together became routine. They each wore a teasing, shy smile as they shared breakfast alone in the kitchen. Abby prepared a feast for Mason to eat while she only sipped a cup of hot tea. She would eat something with Cactus Flower after they had started the noon meal.

Abby had placed all the new furniture in the house and it had taken on a homey atmosphere that Mason loved. He was proud of the job Abby had done in arranging all the furnishings. Every night they sat in the parlor where Mason read his Bible and Abby sat and rested. The bedtime routine for Mason was like preparing for a firing squad. He lingered as long as he could before retiring to the guest room alone, while Abby snuggled under the covers in his new, four-poster bed.

Mason's patience was stretched nearly out of control, because he didn't know how much longer he could wait for her to get used to him. She was a beautiful young woman and he had fallen head over heels in love. He wanted to bury his face in her long, golden curls and kiss her silly. Every night before crawling in bed, he said a silent prayer that she would soon be ready to be his bride. He was trying hard not to break his promise. She would let him know when she was prepared to become his wife.

Weeks passed of pure torture, and Mason stayed in the barn for as long as he could. Hopefully, she would be asleep, but that was not to be. As he crept toward his room in his stocking feet, he found Abby pacing the length of her room. She stopped once and peeked out the window. He leaned up against the door frame watching her. What in Hades was she doing out of bed? He watched and waited for her to notice him.

"Oh, Mason, you gave me a fright. Where have you been and what has happened to your hand?" He had a bloody rag wrapped around his right palm.

"I was digging a splinter from a horse's hoof and I let my blade slip. It sliced my palm, but it's all right now. I stopped the bleeding." He held out his hand displaying the bloody cut.

"Let me see," she said as she rushed to his side. "This is going to need some salve and a proper bandage, and you are all wet. Is it raining?"

Mason stared at Abby as she stood before him in her thin white muslin gown. Her soft white breasts were exposed and the curves of her hips were outlined. Even a blind man would be tempted. "Yes, a storm is coming."

As Mason held out his hand when she returned with the medical basket, he said, "For goodness sakes, Missy. If you're going to doctor me, you'd best cover yourself before I forget myself and toss you on that bed and have my way with you." Beads of sweat popped out on his forehead and upper lip.

"Oh, you, that's no way to ask me to get my robe!" She whirled around and snatched her robe off the bed and put it on, jerking the ties as tight as she could around her waist.

***

Abby couldn't believe that she had lain waiting for Mason to come inside and go to his bed. She loved the way that he had reached out and caressed the side of her face like he had done the first night that he demanded they sleep together. Some nights, like tonight, it seemed like an eternity before he came back from the barn. She had developed strong feelings for this wonderful man.

Many times she would wake and find herself wishing that she could sleep pressed up against his back or place her head on his shoulder. There really wasn't any way she could deny the attraction that flowed through her body. There were nights that she wanted to sneak into his room and snuggle up close to him without waking him. His scent filled her nostrils and made her smile when she was near him. She did want him to make love to her but she wondered if it was just lust. Was she a wanton woman, or maybe worse? Could she be like the ladies who worked for her mama?

Mason's voice brought her out of her deep thoughts as she pinched his skin when her fingernail dug into his hand. "Are your deliberately trying to hurt me?"

"Sorry, I didn't realize how tired I am. We both

should have been asleep a long time ago since we have to get up early." Abby said, as she examined the bandage and announced that she would change it again tomorrow evening.

"You should wear a glove over that hand while you work outside tomorrow."

"I will," he said, looking down at the neat bandage. "Thanks." He slowly started to the door but suddenly stopped and turned. He grabbed Abby and pulled her into his arms. He ran his fingers in her hair and placed his lips over hers. Feeling her body relax, he deepened the kiss. The urgency of holding her was overpowering, and he was afraid that she would pull away from him. The ache in his body was exposed and consuming. He wanted to carry her to bed and ravish her young body, but he only cradled her closer.

A loud clap of thunder ripped near the bedroom window, causing Abby to jump back away from his embrace. They stared at each other. He was stunned at what had just taken place. He knew, even without any words spoken between them, that she liked his caresses.

***

Abby felt weak from head to toe. She had never been kissed like that before, but if this was any indication of how it was, she wanted more, much more. She vaguely remembered Mason leaving her room.

# Chapter 14

Mason worked as hard as his men. They were getting the corrals ready for his new herd of horses. Fences always needed repairing, and with his big herd of cattle that had arrived earlier in the year, branding seemed to be an endless job. Planting oats and corn was a big job and harvesting the crop seemed to be an even bigger task. There were many ranch chores that kept Mason busy all day, every day.

One morning, Abby asked Mason if she could go to the trading post and get a few things. "You don't need to interrupt your work. Cactus Flower and I can walk."

"Abby, you have been here almost a month and this is the first time you have asked for anything. Make a list of items you would like to buy and we'll go as soon as you're ready. Peterson opens early and he has a great many items to choose from since Uncle Jackson shipped supplies here. I know the old men that hang around the post are curious about you," he said as a chuckle escaped from his mouth.

"It will be nice to see another woman besides Cactus Flower. I remember meeting Mrs. Peterson. I look forward to visiting with her again."

"I was hoping the traveling minister would be back in our area soon, but he hasn't returned since we married. Old Peterson holds the church service in the back of his store. I hope one day the trading post will have a building that can be used as a schoolhouse and church."

***

In less than an hour, Mason pulled his large two-seater carriage in front of the house and helped Abby and Cactus Flower up on the seats. They traveled the two miles to the trading post. Abby was surprised to see about a dozen men of all ages milling around the front porch. Two old men with unkempt beards sat on the porch playing checkers, while one or two watched.

When Mason helped Abby down from the carriage, one of the older men spit a stream of tobacco juice, wiped his mouth and tumbled the checker board off the table. The other men watched without blinking an eye. They had heard that young Sunday Boy had a pretty little wife but no one had prepared them for such a beauty.

"Lord have mercy on that boy's soul. He can't be getting any ranching done out at his place with that pretty little gal living with him," one of the men murmured to the others, loud enough for Mason to hear.

"Ain't that the truth," another commented.

Mason watched as Cactus Flower trotted down the path toward the shacks behind the store. He offered Abby his hand as they climbed the few steps to the porch.

"Morning, fellows," he said, as he pulled Abby a little closer to his side. "This is my new bride, Abby, from San Francisco." He smiled at each of the men. "Abby, this here is Abe. He hasn't cut his beard since I've known him," Mason said with a laugh. "This handsome fellow," he said, pointing to an old man who didn't have a tooth in his head, "is Ike. He likes pretty girls, but he's harmless. And the youngest of these fellows is Henry. Several months ago we celebrated his seventy-sixth birthday."

Abby smiled at each of the men as she held onto Mason's arm. The old men looked like they might devour her, so she moved closer to Mason. He noticed and smiled down at her. "Come," he said as he guided her into the store. As they turned to enter the door, all the men jumped to their feet. It didn't escape Mason's attention that the old men followed on their heels into the store. When he glanced in their direction, they pretended to be looking at merchandise. Mason wasn't fooled. He was aware of Abby's shudder as she averted her eyes from the intense stares of the old fellows. They were harmless, but she didn't know that.

Mr. Peterson came in from the back room, and after he said his howdy do's, he bellowed for his wife, Marie. "Get down here, woman. We've got a visitor."

"My lands, husband, you don't have to yell like something is after you. And besides, I ain't deaf," she said as she wiped her hands on her apron.

"Hello again, Mrs. Peterson," Abby said, as she stood holding onto Mason's arm.

"Well, I declare if it isn't the new bride and groom. We were beginning to think that you were holding her prisoner out at your place. It's been near a month since the old preacher man read the vows over ya'll."

"We both have been busy, but I did want to thank you proper-like for standing up for us at our wedding. I'm sure I never said thank you for helping me get ready."

"Honey, that was nothing a'tall. We've all been hoping Mason would get hitched but we did think it would be with Grow Too Tall, who wants to be called Matilda," she said. "She's shore hopping mad at Mason."

"Mason, you never told me that you already had an intended waiting on you," Abby teased.

Mason shifted to give Abby a stern look. "I know you're joking, but it had better end here and now." It was all Abby could do not to laugh at the expression on his face.

"Now Marie, you know good and well I never led that child on or gave her any idea that I was going to marry her." Mason's blushing cheeks and the sweat on his upper lip expressed his discomfort in discussing the Indian girl who chased after him when he came to the trading post.

"I know that, Mason, but that gal was on the warpath when she heard that you had taken a wife. She said that she was going to get back at you for not taking her as your bride. I'm just warning you, just in case you run into her."

Mason took Abby's arm and led her into the back of the store where all kinds of things were scattered about for the women shoppers. "Choose whatever you need or want, but be quick about it. We've got to get back to the ranch."

***

Abby chuckled within with the knowledge that Mason wanted to leave the store before he had to confront the Indian girl who had her hopes set on marrying him. Mason would have to see her eventually but she was sure that he didn't want an audience to witness the confrontation. Abby selected several skeins of white crochet thread and a bolt of material with yellow and white dots. New curtains would certainly brighten up the room. A large piece of yellow oil cloth would look nice on the big kitchen table.

On the short trip home, Abby asked Mason to tell her

about the troubled young Indian girl. His only reply was that her trouble was her own making and left it at that. She knew he was angry by the way he snapped at her and handled the horses.

Mason made it back to the ranch in record time. Why did he feel that he had to race the two horses pulling the carriage? Once, she thought he might turn them over when they flew around a bend in the road.

"Why were you in such a hurry to get back here, Mason? We didn't wait for Cactus Flower to return with us."

"So, I could do this," he said as he grabbed her small shoulders and pulled her close into his arms. He kissed her hard and fast on the lips.

Breathing hard, Abby sighed. "We had an understanding, Mason. You seem to accost me anytime you feel like it. What is your intention if I might ask?" she finished in barely a whisper.

"Why, sweetheart, honorable of course. Wasn't that in our wedding vows? The minister read words like *for better or worse, love and honor till death do us part.*"

"What in tarnation does that have to do with you kissing me out in the front yard for everyone to see? Do you want the men to believe that I'm some fancy tart that came looking for you?"

"Hush that kinda talk right this minute. I just wanted to kiss my wife and I'll kiss you when and where I feel like it. Now go in the house and put lunch together for all the hungry eyes that are watching us." Mason turned on his heels, handed her a package, and led the carriage to the barn, murmuring under his breath.

What a shame that a lovely morning turned into a battle of words with her hardheaded husband, Abby thought as she went to the bedroom to change into a work dress.

# Chapter 15

San Francisco

At The Red Dog Saloon, the old Irish cook, sat at the kitchen table peeling a dozen boiled eggs. "I hate peeling these darn things. I can't believe Abby ran off. She's a stinking, spoiled brat. She could come back and tell me thanks for teaching her to cook. I could have hit her over the head many times with this here wooden spoon, but no, I had to treat her like a little princess."

"You know, old woman, I had big plans for Abby. I practically raised her, you know. I was just waiting 'till she was a little older ABBY I was going to make a fortune with her. Our very own Abigale, the new queen." Lucinda sighed, thinking about the money that she had lost since Abby left to heaven knows where.

"I knew Bella wouldn't be here much longer, with some of the medicine that I was giving her to help her *rest*." Lucinda picked up an egg, attempting to help the cook. Frustrated that the shell wouldn't come off, she finally tossed it in the trash.

"You ain't saying that you gave her *something* to hurry her on to her Maker, are you?" A furrow formed between the old cook's eyebrows.

"Shut your trap and keep a civil tongue in your head. I ain't never harmed Bella," Lucinda replied sharply. She knew the sleeping powder didn't harm Bella, but it didn't help her either.

"Well, why don't you go after our little princess and bring her back home? That old banker sent her to live with some relatives up north of here. She might not be liking it in those woods since she's a city gal."

"You and I think alike—sometimes for sure. Sal said that he's found two young brothers who have run up a big bar bill, and old Henry is ready to toss them in jail. He's going to bring them to see me." The sound of a door banging and heavy boots stomping on the floor made Lucinda glance toward the door. "That sounds like them coming in the front now." Lucinda glared at the old cook and told her to keep her trap shut. "Let me do all the talking."

Two young men stood in front of Lucinda and listened to her demands. The oldest brother questioned her. "You want us to do what?"

"You heard what I said. You boys know who I'm

talking about, too. Don't stand in front of me acting dumb as old mules. Every man alive in this city has heard about Abby Mills—her beauty, if nothing else. Now, they know her mama's died."

"Sure we heard, but she left the city headed to northern California. That's what we heard."

"Yes, she has and if you two value your lives, you'll make the trip up there and bring her back here. She wants to come home, and I need you two to go and get her. Do I make myself clear?"

Willie looked at his brother, Sandy, and lifted his shoulders. "What do you think, brother?"

"It don't matter what he thinks." Sal stepped between the two Jordon brothers, lacing his big fists around the back of their necks.

"I heard that Mr. Bridges, the postmaster, needs someone to carry the mail bags to towns, villages and trading posts that are on the way to Eagle's Station, where Abby is living now. This will be your excuse for arriving in the village. You shouldn't have any trouble in locating the backwoods where Abby was taken," Lucinda said as she peeled apples. "I hate doing this." She looked at the cook and frowned.

"What will you pay us for bringing her back here— to you?" Willie asked trying to squirm away from the bouncer.

"What'd you think, Sal? Should we let them live and allow them to settle their debt to us?" Lucinda said as she slammed the knife down on the counter and glared at the young man. "You see, we don't like freeloaders hanging around our saloon. Bad for business, you understand?"

Lucinda glared at the young men as their faces turned pale. Reaching her hand into her bosom, she pulled out a few dollars. Tossing the money on the table, she said, "Go down to the store and get a few supplies, then be on your way after you stop in and see Mr. Bridges. Don't try anything, like not doing this job. Sal has eyes everywhere and you'll be sorry if you disappoint me."

***

Willie and Sandy Jordon packed their saddlebags with their meager supplies and headed out of San Francisco. It seemed that every man's eyes were watching them as they headed out of town on their mission. There was no way they could go in a different direction because they had heard tell of other men disappearing after being hired by Sal, the bouncer at The Red Dog Saloon.

The two young men were thankful that the weather had been good and the trail to the trading post in Eagle's Station was smooth and clear. Many freight wagons, covered wagons and riders traveled on the trail to Northern California. The two brothers made good time and enjoyed stopping in the towns and villages to deliver mail. Everyone who collected it was pleased and offered to feed them and their horses.

After arriving in Eagle's Station, they located the trading post. Mr. Peterson seemed pleased to see the delivery of the mail. They tossed their saddlebags on the counter and removed the letters and packages from San Francisco. Villagers had been waiting months, especially Mason. Peterson had been anxiously waiting on the *San Francisco Tribute.* Customers would pay a penny to read the paper. He had a stack of letters to be sent back, but the two brothers said that they weren't hired to take mail back, but they guessed they might be able to oblige him.

After taking their horses to the livery, they asked the Smithy if there was a place they could bunk down for a night or two.

"I got a couple of cots in the back. I charge fifty cents a night. You have to use your own bedrolls."

After squaring up with the big man, the two brothers walked to Peterson's Trading Post and sat on the porch steps. The old men that were playing checkers couldn't stop talking about the Sunday Boy's new wife.

"That's shore one pretty filly, if I say so myself." Abe commented as he spit a stream of tobacco juice at the feet of one of the brothers.

"Hey old man, watch where you spitting or I'll come up there and make you swallow that plug," he snarled. The old man kept right on talking and playing checkers. With a double barrel shotgun lying at his feet, he didn't seem scared of the two whippersnappers.

"That boy shore waited long enough for her, but I'd

say it was worth the wait. Man, she's a little beauty." Ike said, taking his red checker and jumping his partner's black one. "Crown me, old man," he hooted with laughter.

Willie and Sandy Jordon smirked at each other. Their eyes signaled that they had found the pretty girl, Abby. They sauntered into the trading post to get something to eat.

"I'm gonna ride out to Mason's and give him this mail. Poor fellow has waited months to hear from his uncle," Peterson said to his wife as he held several envelopes. "I'll be back within the half hour."

The two men wandered around the store selecting cheese and apples. They watched and waited until the store owner had left the area before they asked about Abby Mills. "Madam, do you know of a young woman by the name of Abby Mills who might live somewhere near here?"

"Her name ain't Mills no more. It's Waters now. She up and married Mason Waters about a month or so ago."

"You don't say. Gosh, I'd better get on back to where I come from then." Sandy frowned and looked downright pitiful. "I was hoping that she would have married me."

"Oh Sandy, I'm sorry. I shore thought she was going to wait on you." Willie patted his brother on his back. "Hey, maybe we could stop and say hello to her and congratulate them."

"I think that's a wonderful idea. I'm sure Abby would love to see someone from home." Having second thoughts, Mrs. Peterson's eyes narrowed at the two young men. "You aren't going to make a fuss because she married Mason, are you?"

"Oh, no ma'am. Abby is an old friend. I'm happy for her if she is happy with this man she married." Sandy glanced at Willie and grinned.

"Well, all right. Go down that road about two miles. They have a nice ranch house on the right. You can't miss it." Marie followed the two young men onto the porch and waved goodbye.

# Chapter 16

Abby prepared the food for lunch and left it on the stove for Cactus Flower to finish cooking later. Dressed in her trousers, she gathered her garden tools, gloves and bonnet. She wanted to plant a few rows of green beans, a row of peppers and some tomato plants. Joey and Buster had already planted several rows of potatoes, carrots, and cucumbers. Many of the plants were already about a foot high, but weeds were threatening to take over the garden. Abby got down on her knees and started weeding.

Mr. Peterson rode his big Appaloosa horse up to the front of the house and tossed his reins over the hitching post. Abby removed her gloves and strode to the corner of the house and called to him. "I'm here, Mr. Peterson."

"Afternoon, Mrs. Waters," he said, his eyes wide as he noticed her wearing trousers. "Is Mason at home?"

"I'm afraid not. He's out in the north pasture with his men. I believe they're mending some of the fences," she replied as she gazed at his horse.

"You have a beautiful mount. What kind of horse is it? I've never seen a horse that looks like a leopard before."

"Have you ever seen a leopard, Mrs. Waters?"

"No," she smiled at him. "As a child, I read many books and I have always loved different animals."

"My horse is an Appaloosa and I bought him off a couple that needed money to keep traveling to the gold fields. I think I got the better of that deal," he said with a wink.

"Well, he's big and certainly is different-looking. I think he's lovely, if you can say that about a horse. May I get you some refreshment before you have to get back to the store?"

"Just give this mail to Mason. I believe there's a letter from his uncle. I'd better get on back to Marie. She don't like staying alone at the post."

"Thank you so much for bringing this out to us. I know Mason will appreciate it." Abby wiped the sweat off her forehead with her gloves, which smeared dirt on her face.

"Don't be a stranger now, you hear. Marie enjoys your visits."

Abby carried the mail into the kitchen and placed it

on the table where Mason always sat to have his dinner. She drank a dipper of fresh water and returned outside to complete her task in the garden.

Abby bent down as she carefully pulled weeds away from the potato plants. She picked nasty bugs off the leaves and placed them in a jar, not having the heart to kill them, but she didn't want to turn them lose to jump on other plants. Wiping sweat off her forehead, she heard footsteps behind her and without looking, she called out to Mason.

"Hello, Mason, Mr. Peterson came by and left some mail for you. I put it in the house." When he didn't answer, she turned and shaded her eyes to see him better, but it wasn't her husband.

Abby bolted to her feet as two strangers approached too close to her for comfort.

"Who are you?" she asked, hoping her voice didn't tremble. For some reason, she felt uncomfortable.

One of the young men wouldn't stop staring at her. Her arms crossed her chest like a shield. She searched for someone—anyone to come to her aid.

When the two men didn't answer her, a bad feeling flowed through her body. Stay calm, she said to herself. "If you want to water your horses, there's water over by the barn. Help yourselves."

Neither man said anything in response. Abby tried to walk around them and move closer to the back porch.

One of the young men stepped in front of the other and reached for Abby's arm. She slapped his hand away with the garden tool that she held in her hand. "Hey, that hurt!"

"There'll be more of that if you touch me again. So, if you don't want to water your horses, it's best you be on your way and leave this ranch. My husband and his men will be here any minute, and my husband won't like you trying to touch me," Abby said firmly.

The one who'd been staring at her spoke as she took a step backward from them. "My name's Sandy. Look, Miss Lucinda said that you wanted to return to San Francisco, so she sent me and my brother Willie to fetch you home. If you will please come with us, we'll have you home in about a week."

Abby couldn't believe his words. She was confused.

"I'm sorry you both have traveled a long way, but I have no desire to return to San Francisco, much less to The Red Dog Saloon. There is nothing there for me now that my mama has passed away. I don't know why Lucinda would have sent you all this way after me. Besides, I'm married now. I don't want to leave my husband or my new home."

"You must come back with us." Willie took a step toward her.

She frowned at the men while she tried to make sense out of why Lucinda had sent them after her. "I've already told you both that I don't intend to go with you. I am sorry that you made this long trip, but I must bid you goodbye. I have to go in and finish preparing lunch. The men will be here soon and they'll expect food on the table."

Abby had to escape the two men who seemed almost desperate to make her go with them. They were scaring her and she prayed that Mason and the men would return home soon for lunch.

Abby turned to walk away from the garden when the one called Willie grabbed her arm and twisted it back behind her. He started pushing her toward the barn. "Sorry, little girl, but you're coming along with us."

Too late, Abby knew they were taking her to the barn to get a horse. God help her. She wished she had listened to her instinct sooner because something told her that these men were up to no good. No one had ever manhandled her before and she was scared. She had to come up with a way to get away from them before they tied her hands.

"Hold her," Willie said, as he pushed her into Sandy's arms while he tossed a lead rope around a horse and led him out of the stall. Then he tossed the horse's rope to Sandy as he looked for a blanket and saddle.

Willie called to him to bring her and the horse over to him.

Sandy pulled on the animal's rope, but he tossed his head and walked backwards. He pawed the ground and wouldn't move. Sandy turned his back on Abby as he pulled harder on the bridle. Abby saw her only chance to run. She raced to the back of the barn and hurried out the back door. Then she raced into the woods behind the outhouse.

***

Sandy was stunned at first that she had gotten out of his reach so fast. He hurried after her, but she darted and twisted in the underbrush, making it harder for him to catch her. And those trousers made it easier for her maneuver through the brush.

Willie and Sandy went searching deeper into the woods and veered off in different directions, hoping to capture her.

***

After running for a long time, she had to stop and rest for a second. With a stitch in her side, she stooped down as low as she could but continued to head further away from the ranch and deeper into the forest. Bending over and breathing hard, she was sure that she had lost them. She listened for any sign of the men.

Then the earth fell out from under her.

She screamed for help, but all she heard was her own voice echoing until her small body landed at the bottom of a pit.

***

"Willie," Sandy called. "Over here. We've got her now."

Willie rushed to Sandy's side, breathing hard and fast. "You'd better be glad you caught her. Why did you let her get away to begin with?"

"Never mind, we've got her now. Come and help me get her out of her hiding place."

As the two men looked down into the hole where Abby had disappeared, they couldn't believe their eyes. "Oh, Lord, Willie, she's fallen into an abandoned pit. How are we going to get her?"

"Let me light a match and we'll be able to see how deep this thing might be." He struck a small match, but it wasn't enough light to shine into the pit. "Make a torch out of some branches so we can see her better. You know there isn't a sound coming from down there. Reckon she's just being quiet so we'll go away?" Sandy said.

Willie poked the torch down inside the dark pit which shed a luminous glow to the walls. Lying at the bottom of the hole, which appeared to be about fifteen feet deep, was a lifeless body. She had landed face down on her stomach, but her head was lying sideways on the muddy earth. One leg was twisted to the side. Just then, a giant snake, awakened from its nest, coiled and raised its head. Willie pulled his pistol and fired one shot, blowing the head off the snake. Even after the blast of the gun, Abby's body didn't move.

"Damn, Willie, you've killed her!" Sandy grabbed his brother around the neck and slung him on the ground. With both hands wrapped around his neck, he screamed while shaking his brother almost lifeless. Slowly Willie's fist connected with a small limb and he managed to slam it on Sandy's head. With all the strength Willie had left, he shoved his wild brother off him and stood up.

"You crazy fool," he said, coughing, while rubbing his neck. "I wasn't aiming at the girl. I shot a snake that was crawling near her body."

"Oh, Willie, I'm sorry, but I believe she's dead. We killed her for sure. What're we goin' do? She was so beautiful and now we killed her."

"You killed her, if anyone did by letting her escape from the barn! I ain't going to hang because of your stupidity."

"That's a lie," Sandy screamed as he grabbed the front of his brother's vest and pulled his face close. "She ran and we couldn't catch her. I'd never harm a hair on her head. Besides, we don't have to let anyone know that we were chasing her. We don't have to return to San Francisco. We can just keeping going to Canada."

"Listen to me, little brother. The hole is real deep and we ain't got a rope that will reach down to her. We can't get her out by ourselves. You're right about one thing. We can't afford to let anyone know that we know she's in this hole. Come on. Let's get back to the livery and clean up. We'll go back to the trading post and get something to eat. Keep our ears open to see if she comes up missing. Maybe her husband will think she ran off by herself."

Willie wanted to return to San Francisco and tell

Lucinda that the girl had run away and that no one had any idea where she went. That would get them out of trouble with that old hag and the big man who worked for her.

"But Willie, what if she wakes up? It's so dark down there and she's all alone."

"If they find her alive, we'll shore have to skedaddle and be quick about it. She'll tell them that we tried to take her back to Lucinda and then they'll hang us for kidnapping." Willie gave his brother's shoulders a good shake. "Get ahold of yourself and let me do all the talking if someone asks us anything."

# Chapter 17

The ranch hands had gathered around the water trough washing and splashing each other with the cool water. They'd worked hard after breakfast, repairing and replacing fence boards.

Buster was wiping his hands dry when he noticed something strange. "Look yonder, fellows. There's a horse out of the barn and it's grazing in the front yard. I sure hope he hasn't gotten into the new kitchen garden." Tossing his drying cloth down on the ground, he raced after the animal.

As Buster led the horse back to the barn, he noticed a saddle and horse blanket lying on the barn floor. The saddle had been in the tack room that morning.

"Mr. Waters," Buster called, as the boss headed toward the back porch of the house. Mason turned to the young man.

"Buster, how many times do I have to tell you to call me Mason?"

"Sorry, sir, but something ain't right. Someone has been messing around in the barn since we left this morning. That workhorse of yours was wandering around in the yard. A saddle and blanket are lying on the barn floor and a bridle is hanging on a post in a stall instead of being in the tack room."

"Show me."

Mason followed Buster into the barn, and the equipment was lying all around just as Buster had described. The men knew that everything on the ranch had a place. Equipment was expensive and even the smallest tool needed to be cared for and put away.

Mason knew that none of his men had left the saddle and blanket on the dirty floor and he couldn't imagine Abby attempting to ride a horse because he hadn't had time to give her riding lessons. Besides, she couldn't lift that heavy saddle onto a horse's back.

Without a word, Mason hurried across the yard to check on his young wife. He hoped she hadn't attempted to leave him again. Cactus Flower was standing at the stove, spooning gravy over a big pork roast when he looked in the kitchen.

"Where's Abby?"

"Gone." Her reply was simple without any regard to Mason's concern.

Mason raced down the hall to Abby's bedroom. The

room was neat and her soft slippers were on the floor next to the bed. He opened the dresser drawers, and her clothes and personal items were there. Nothing appeared to be missing.

"Cactus Flower, how long have you been here? Was Abby here when you arrived?"

"I come a while ago. I sat and waited. She not come. I finished cooking food that she left on the stove. Lunch is ready to eat."

A pounding at the back door made Mason swivel in its direction, and he yelled to come in. Joey stood with his hat in his hand, twisting it around and around.

"What is it, Joey?" Mason asked with a growl.

"Something is sure wrong, sir. Mrs. Waters or someone had worked in the small garden this morning. There are fresh weeds pulled and the hoe and shovel are just lying about. I found this small glove next to the privy, and there looks to be several fresh horse tracks. None of us rode that way."

Mason could feel the blood draining out of his face and his gut felt as if someone was twisting a knife in it. "Go gather the men for me. Abby isn't here, and I'd bet my last dollar that she didn't leave the ranch alone. Send Buster to the trading post and see if she's been there this morning."

"Yes sir." Joey replied, as he backed out of the kitchen, pushing the screen door open with his backside. He scampered down the steps yelling at the top of his lungs for Buster to come.

Mason studied Cactus Flower who stood at the stove. "When you got here this morning, did you see Abby outside in the garden?"

"No, but I did see the barn door open and I walked over and pushed the door shut. I know you don't like it open when all the men are gone." She replaced the lids on top of the food. It didn't look like the men were going to eat anytime soon.

As the men gathered on the back porch, Mason gave them instructions to search every inch of the ground and then they would go in pairs into the woods behind the ranch. "It's possible that if she was taken by force, they might have followed the path through the woods to the main trail."

***

The men began to search the ranch. Wilson, an older ranch hand, was sure he found fresh boot prints that were much smaller than the average man's. There were several other prints too, but much larger. He called Mason to examine the footprints.

"Do you think that Mrs. Waters would be wearing boots today?"

"If she was going to work in the garden, I'm sure she wouldn't be wearing her soft house slippers. Yes, I'm sure she would be wearing her boots."

"Buster and Joey are the smallest men working here, but I'm sure that these prints aren't theirs, too small for one thing." Wilson bent down on one knee and cleaned the area surrounding the tracks.

"Here is the smaller boot print. It appears that the person wearing these boots was in a big hurry because the prints are wide apart, like they're running. The larger prints are going in the same direction but they appear to be standing, and then the tracks are further apart as they go off into the woods."

"Are you thinking that Abby might have run out of the barn into the woods?"

"Yep, that's what it looks like to me."

Mason hurried to the back door of the ranch house and rang the dinner bell. The men gathered quickly as Buster rode into the yard.

"She ain't been at the trading post, but Mr. Peterson's wife said that two young men were asking about her earlier," Buster said, as he jumped down from his hot sweaty animal.

"Men it looks like my wife has been taken from the ranch by force, but it is possible that she escaped and ran off into the woods. Wilson found several sets of boot prints. We could be out searching for hours. Take your canteens filled with fresh water. If you find her, signal by firing your gun twice in the air. Hurry now and get prepare to leave."

Mason went to his bedroom and closed the door. He sat down on his bed, held his head in his hands and prayed.

*Oh Lord, please help us find Abby safe. Please help me bring her home. I know that I already have strong feelings for this lovely young woman that you have allowed into my life. I promise to love and protect her with everything I have. Please guide us to her. Amen*

When Mason returned to the kitchen, Cactus Flower offered him a sandwich, but he waved it away. "Coffee is all I want."

The men were waiting for Mason when he came outside. "Let's spread out in the woods and search in groups of twos."

"Mason, you know old Abe. Well, he has a set of good hunting dogs. I bet we could set them on her trail. Why don't I go into the village and ask him to bring them over?"

Mason knew if she could be found, Abe's dogs could do the trick.

"Hurry, we need everyone out searching. It will be dark in a few hours."

---

## Chapter 18

---

Back at the trading post. . .

Land sakes, Paul! It's been a month of Sundays since you passed this way. Good to see you, man. You got a job near here?" Mr. Peterson asked as he pounded the older lumberjack, Paul Miller, on the back.

"Almost didn't recognize the place," the big lumberjack said as he surveyed the room. It sure has grown since I was here last. Your store looks mighty fine, and it's filled to the brim with almost everything a man out this way could want."

"Mason Waters' uncle and I are in business together. He ships me the supplies and I sell them on commission. Right good deal for me, if I do say so myself."

"Mason sent for my men and me a few months ago. It took us awhile to complete our other job. I hope he still wants our help. He wrote that he needed more land cleared for grazing."

"I'm sure he'll be happy to see you. You know that young Sunday Boy has taken himself a bride, and man, she's a little beauty. His uncle sent her from San Francisco to marry up with him—like a mail-order bride. Funny thing, too, her being so young and pretty."

"It's a little late for me to be calling on Mason this evening. I'll get my men and set up our tents. Mind if we set up in the back of your post like before?"

"Help yourself to the water pump and privy out there," Peterson said and he headed back into the store.

***

Paul Miller approached several men who sat on the wagon that contained all types of equipment for cutting down trees. His eyes landed on the medical bag sitting next to some axes.

Paul had not always been a lumberjack. As a young man straight out of medical school, he fell in love and married. His first practice was in San Francisco. One day he was called away from the city to care for some miners in the hills. He remember that was the day his luck turned south.  He got caught in a gold mine explosion and buried alive for many weeks. After being cared for by a family for months, his luck turned south again when he returned to San Francisco to his wife and little girl. Once he arrived home, he discovered that his wife had been unfaithful to him. He packed his belongings and left Sin City. Later, he didn't blame his wife. How could she have known he was stuck in that gold mind?

After months of recovery, he decided that he never wanted to work in the medical field again. After meeting the owner of the McQueen Lumber Company, he begged him to let him work and train to become a lumberjack. With his size, a man over six foot and muscular, the owner agreed to give him the opportunity to learn.

As the years passed by and the demand for more lumberjacks grew, Paul started his own company in Northern California and Oregon. He enjoyed the freedom of being his own boss and not having to be accountable to anyone but his faithful employees. But not a day went by that he didn't think about his wife and daughter. Were they safe? Were they happy?

Paul waved to his men for them to follow him behind the store and prepare their tents and build a fire. They tied their horses to a picket line and settled around the campfire to rest.

***

Abe arrived at Mason's barn with his two black and white coonhounds. "These two hounds can sniff out a rabbit buried in a gopher's hole that's at least ten-feet-deep." Abe spit a stream of tobacco juice six feet. "Let me have that thar glove of your young bride so my dogs can get a good whiff. They'll be off like lightning, so be ready to follow them."

Mason gave Abe the glove, and within seconds, Abe's two hounds were around the barn and out into the woods before any of the men could even turn around.

"Git going!" Abe yelled. "I'm coming too, but I'm a mite slower than the rest of you fellows."

Mason and his men followed the dogs for hours into the woods. The sun had settled and the dogs lay resting in a bed of tall weeds. Cactus Flower rode her horse toward the group of men who were trying to decide which way Abby may have run. She carried a basket of sandwiches and a bag of small apples for the men to eat.

"Thanks, Cactus Flower. I know the men will appreciate a little something to eat." Mason smiled at the old Indian woman and took the basket from her.

"Mrs. Marie said that those two men who asked about your woman are sleeping in the back of the livery stable," Cactus Flower said.

"Mick," Mason called to his foreman. "I'm going to the trading post and speak with those two men. Please keep the dogs and the men searching. I'll be back as soon as I can."

Mason strode to Cactus Flower and asked if she would ride double with him back to the house. She scooted down off her horse allowing Mason to get on. He grabbed her arm and swung her up behind him. They rode to the house where he raced to saddle his big bay and continue on to the post.

Mason peeked in the back room of the livery. A young man was sitting on a bunk bed drinking from a whiskey bottle. He was talking to the other man who had his head covered with a pillow. Mason couldn't make out anything the man was saying.

Mason circled to the front of the livery and knocked softly on Smithy's door. The next thing he knew, Smithy was pointing a double-barreled shotgun in his face.

"Hold on there, fellow." Mason raised his two arms. "It's just me, Mason."

Smithy lowered the gun and waved for him to enter his living area. "What in the blazing are you doing out this time of night?"

"Haven't you heard that my wife is missing?"

"Yep, but I figured she'd got tired of you and ran off again." He smiled at his own joke.

"No, this time she was chased away from the ranch by two men. I believe those two fellows sleeping in your stable know something. I want you to come with me while I question them. Bring that cannon with you," Mason said, pointing to the big shotgun.

As Mason and Smithy crept to the back of the stable, someone was saying he was sure that they killed the girl. Mason nearly fell to his knees when he heard that statement.

"Come on, Mason. Buck up, old man, and let's grab them while we still can," Smithy said as he led the way into the back.

"Hey fellows," Smithy said, pointing his shotgun in the direction of the two young men. "We want to ask you a few questions."

Mason jerked the drunken man off his bunk. "Where's Abby? Where is my wife?" He shook the man so hard his teeth were rattling.

"Mason, settle down. Give him a chance to answer," Smithy demanded.

Mason dropped the man back on the cot and waited.

"I don't know for sure, but she's out there in the woods in a big hole. *He* killed her for sure!"

Pointing to the one who'd just spoken, the younger one screamed, "He did it," and started crying.

"Can't you see the young fool is drunk? He's talking out of his head. We don't know nothing about your wife. " The older one said, as he sat up and straightened his clothes.

"You're lying and you know it. Both of you are going to hang first thing in the morning if you don't tell me right this second what you did with her," Mason enunciated each word through gritted teeth.

"Willie, tell them. I don't want to hang. We didn't mean for her to fall in that pit. Please, Willie." The younger man grabbed the front of other one's shirt.

"Shut your fool mouth, brother. If anyone hangs, it will be you. You let her get away and chased her until she fell. You, not me!"

Mason grabbed the older one and pushed him to the

door. "Show me where you left her to die. Now, before I hang both of you myself."

Willie must have read the wild look in Mason's eyes because he said, "All right, all right, we'll do our best to show you where she fell. We ran around and around in the woods so it might not be easy to find her."

"You'll find the spot or I don't know what I will do." Mason's big hands grabbed the older brother and shook him again, almost lifting him up off the floor.

Smithy hurried and saddled up two horses. They made the two brothers ride together while they led their horses in the direction of Mason's barn. After hours of searching the woods, the one named Sandy remembered seeing a particular tree and he yelled, "She's over there."

Some of the men who were following dogs joined them. The coonhounds raced forward and began barking their heads off, circling a big hole in the ground. A lady's bonnet lay on the ground by the hole.

The sun was rising behind the trees as Mason leaned down and peered into the dark pit. "Light me a torch!" he said as he held the bonnet to his chest.

Bunches of tree branches were made into torches and the men gathered around the area to look down into the pit. Lying with her head turned sideways, one foot twisted to the side, Abby lay as still as death.

"Let me go down there, Mason," Joey said. "I'm the smallest."

"Mick, we need ropes and a few straight boards,"

Mason calmly said. "Hurry to the barn and come back in the flatbed wagon with plenty of quilts,too."

***

As Mick rode into the corral area, Paul Miller and a few of his men were walking into the yard.

"Morning!" Paul called to Mick, but Paul could tell by the way the man was rushing around that something was wrong.

"Where's Mason this morning?" Paul asked, trying again to get the man's attention.

"Listen, we've got trouble. Mason's wife is down in a hole and we've got to get her out. I've come for ropes, boards and quilts. Please come back another time."

"Hold on, man. We can help," Paul replied, glancing over his shoulder at his men.

Once Mick had collected all the items that Mason had requested, Paul and his men jumped on the back of the flatbed wagon and rode to the site where Abby had fallen.

"Mason," Paul said as he pushed his way to the front of the pit where Mason stood. "My men and I can help you get her out."

"Praise the Lord, Paul. I'm so happy to see you. Abby, my wife, is down there. It looks to be about a fifteen-foot drop. Joey is in the hole with her. We dropped him down with a short rope. He says she's alive because he can feel a pulse."

Paul knelt and looked down at Joey and Abby. "Grab

one of the quilts and give it to me." Somebody placed a quilt in his hands.

"Joey, I'm tossing down a quilt. Cover the girl with it. We want to get her warm as quickly as we can. Move against the wall of the pit because I'm coming down. I will need you to help me place her on boards so we can lift her out of there."

"Paul, I want to go down after my wife. I'm younger than you."

"I am older, that much is true, but I'm a lumberjack. I can climb up the sides as we lift her. You can't do that. Please move away from the opening so my men can lower me down as I hold onto the sides of the hole."

As Paul's feet hit the muddy bottom next to Abby's body, Joey's eyes were as big as saucers. "What's wrong, young man?" Paul asked.

"There's a snake and several large spiders darting in and out of the big roots," he said, trying not to appear afraid.

Paul scanned the area. "The snake doesn't have a head and the spiders are harmless if you leave them alone. Now, get yourself together and help me."

"Catch the two wide boards that are being lowered and stand them up against the wall while I examine her body."

Paul felt Abby's pulse and ran his hands around her neck and over her arms and legs. Her left foot was swollen. Thank goodness she had lost her boot along the way and she wasn't wearing it. As he gently inched her over onto her back, he saw a large swollen knot on the side of her forehead. He ran his hand over the knot and felt swelling behind her right ear, too. Lucky man, though Paul, to have such a lovely young woman for a spouse. A memory of his wife flashed in his mind.

Paul prayed silently that she didn't have any permanent brain injury from the long fall. He took the two boards from against the wall and wrapped a rope securing them together. He requested another quilt be dropped down to him. He laid the quilt on the boards and told Joey to slide Abby's legs and feet on the boards. He gently lifted her head, shoulders and back onto the boards at the same time. Taking a quilt, he covered her up again with it. Using some of the same rope, he secured Abby on the boards like a mummy.

With another rope, he made a sling, securing it to the boards. When Abby was lifted into the air, she'd stay attached to the straight boards.

"Ready at the top?" Paul yelled. "I'm sending Joey back up first. The rope is tied under his armpits so he should come straight up. Get ready to lift him out."

In a matter of minutes, Joey was back up. Mason grabbed the boy and hugged him tightly. "Thanks, son," he said with tears in his eyes.

"Are you ready to pull us up?" Paul yelled from below. "I'll hold the boards as straight as I can until we get to the very top and then I'll tilt them at the opening. Be very careful the girl doesn't slip."

It seemed like hours passed before Paul and Abby were pulled to safety. As Abby's body appeared at the top of the opening, the men applauded and cheered. She was placed gently on the ground, then lifted and carried to the back of the flatbed wagon as several men helped pull Paul out of the hole. Chunks of dirt could be heard falling to the bottom of the pit. Paul had spread his big boots wide apart and walked up the sides as if he were climbing a tree.

Joey was already settled on the bench of the flatbed wagon, ready to take Mason and Abby home.

***

Mason called his thanks to all the men. He wanted to get Abby home and have the Old Wise Woman check her over. He was holding Abby's head in his lap, brushing the dirty hair away from her lovely face. Mud was caked dry on her cheeks and a significant bump had already formed on the side of her forehead.

"I'll be at the house in a few minutes," Paul called to him as Mason drove away with his wife.

"Buster, please go get the Old Wise Woman and ask her to come and help Abby," said Mason to the young boy.

Mason was speaking to a ranch hand when Paul entered the hallway.

"Mason, we have known each other for a couple of years, but not many people know that before I became a lumberjack, I was a doctor. I would appreciate it if you wouldn't tell anyone. I'll be happy to check your wife and make sure she doesn't have any serious injuries. Please come into the room with me."

Mason was stunned. He had known this man for at least two years and worked beside him while Paul and his crew cut down acres of trees. He couldn't believe that this godly man had such a secret past.

"Certainly, I want Abby to have excellent care. I've sent for the Old Wise Woman. She is the only medical help we have in these parts."

"I'm sure she can help, but I know about broken bones and head injuries. Ask your Indian lady to bring in plenty of hot water."

As Paul disappeared into Abby's room, loud voices came from the back of his house. Smithy appeared on the back porch. He had the two brothers tied together. Several of Mason's men and Paul's lumberjacks were making loud threatening remarks to the boys. As Mason joined his men and glanced at the two, he asked Smithy if he would place a guard on them until he had time to question them. He wanted to get to the bottom of this kidnapping.

"I'll pay good money for the guard you choose to stay the night. I should be able to talk with them tomorrow. After I hear what they were planning, I'll decide what we should do. In the meantime, lock them in the bunkhouse behind the livery."

"Whatever you say, Mason." Smithy pulled the two men behind the horse as they struggled to stand upright.

# Chapter 19

After Abby was carried into her bedroom, Mason placed a fire under the tea kettle so there would be fresh hot water to clean her.

The sun had risen but there was a chill in the air. He tossed several logs in the fireplace in the kitchen.

The men had laid Abby's carrier on the bed and left the room. Paul and Mason removed her from the boards and laid her flat on the mattress. Mason covered her as Joey carried in a big bowl of steaming water and placed it on the table beside the bed. He held a stack of clean rags across his arm and quickly set them down near Abby.

"If I can do anything else, Mason, please just say so. I will be in the next room." Joey said with tears forming in his eyes.

"You did good, son. I'll let you know if I need anything."

"Place one of those rags in the water and give it to me," Paul said, as he ran his hands through Abby's hair. "I need more light in here, too." Mason quickly responded to Paul's demands and stood watch over his young bride.

Paul placed the warm rag on Abby's mud-caked cheeks. As he cleaned her face, a memory of his pretty young wife flashed before his eyes. This beautiful girl was the mirror image of Bella, his wife of three years, who had betrayed him while he was trying to survive in a cave. The only thing that had kept him alive was loving memories of his wife and darling child.

Now, lying before him was a young woman who could be Bella if she was only twenty years younger. Could this be his long-lost daughter?

Memories abounded of the last time he saw his wife. After he'd recovered from nearly starving to death and dehydration, he returned to town. Several people said that he could find his wife working at the saloon. He raced up the saloon's stairs, knocked and went into the room before he was told to enter. His lovely wife was standing beside a rumpled bed, and a big tanned cowboy was lying in the bed, covered from his waist down. The man bellowed as he pulled on Bella's right hand. "Get out of here, you fool, this is my hour!"

She looked as beautiful as the day he had left her to go to the mines and help the miners who had been hurt during the explosion.

"Paul, are you all right?" Mason asked as he noticed all the color had drained from his friend's face. Paul's hands were shaking and he appeared white as a sheet.

"Can you tell how bad Abby is hurt? Will she be okay? What about the swollen place on her head?"

"No, yes, and no, son. As far as I can tell without undressing her, she appears to be okay. When the Old Wise Woman gets here, she can help me with an overall examination. She can bathe her, which will be a big help."

It wasn't long before the two old Indian women arrived. The Old Wise Woman hurried into the bedroom to help Paul while Cactus Flower went to the kitchen to prepare lunch for the men.

***

Breakfast was the quickest meal to prepare so she began whipping up biscuits, bacon, and eggs. She gathered everything to make a big pot of oatmeal. Abby always cooked lunch and dinner for the men, but they would have to do with her cooking for a while. Breakfast food served for lunch would be better than having to wait several hours.

The men had gathered around the back porch. They were waiting for Mason to come out and give them a report about his wife. Abby had won the ranch hands' hearts because she was kind to everyone and a wonderful cook. She seemed to enjoy cooking for them by preparing different pies and her delicious hot cinnamon rolls. The men enjoyed helping her with chores. She always thanked them with sweet words and a smile.

As they waited outside, Cactus Flower could hear them grumbling under their breath among each other. She hoped the girl was going to be all right because it had been years since the area had a hanging, much less two.

Maybe after the men had a full stomach and a nap, they'd settle down. She rang the bell and all the men filed into the kitchen. There was no conversation or joking as they ate and waited to hear news about Abby.

*****

The Old Wise Woman helped remove Abby's dirty clothes and washed every inch of her body. Several pans of hot water were carried back and forth into the room.

Paul felt her arms and legs for broken bones but found none. Her left foot was swollen, but it wasn't broken. He wrapped a tight bandage around her ankle. The worst injury she had was the swollen knot on the side of her forehead. It would turn black and blue soon and she would most likely have a black eye, too. Her ribs were bruised from the fall, but he didn't think any of them were cracked or broken. She didn't have trouble breathing. Paul's biggest concern was her state of unconsciousness. He hoped she would wake up on her own in the next few hours.

Abby looked like an angel lying on the bed with her golden hair spread out on the pillowcase. Paul was still shaking from the knowledge that this woman might be his daughter. He was going to have to wait until she woke up before he got any answers.

***

The Old Wise Woman didn't know Paul, but she had heard about him from some of the other male tribe members. It was said that he might want to hire some of the younger boys to help carry away small limbs and clear the land once the trees were cut down. She hoped that he would hire them as they could use the money to support their families who lived nearby.

"Get into kitchen and eat. I smell the food and I know you and Mason are hungry. We have long night while waiting for Mason's woman to wake."

"Thank you, but please call me Paul. I'm Paul Miller from all over. I'm here to help Mason cut ten acres of trees for more grazing land. I'm sure we'll see each other again."

As the Old Wise Woman sat in Abby's rocker and watched for the smallest movement from the young girl, she remembered what the old lumberjack had said. *He came from all over*. This made her remember that she and some others like her had come from all over, too. They had come down out of the hills of Upper California, and some others had come from as far as the mountains in Oregon.

But it hadn't been easy for her people. The Shastain Indian Tribe was a small one, since most of them had died from cholera. After burying the people, she and some other tribe members set out for a better place to live. After enduring all kinds of weather and near starvation, they settled near Eagle's Station. Mr. Peterson had a small trading post and he said if the Shastain people were a friendly bunch, they could camp out in the woods behind his place.

Shastain means teacher, which described the Old Wise Woman perfectly. She liked to teach the children and doctor all the sick people that came to her. Because of her doctoring, she was well-respected by her people and the white families that lived close by. She shared a small cabin in the woods behind the trading post with her fifteen-year-old son, Running Deer.

The Old Wise Woman also cared for two small children who belonged to a young couple who had died. Running Deer had gotten his name when he was just a young boy because he could run a deer into the ground. Without a bow and arrow or bullets for his rifle, he did whatever it took to bring food home to her table.

She smiled as she thought of her son, who was a young man now, and how good he was to her and the other tribe members. The Indian tribe had laws to live by, and one of the rules was to give assistance and show kindness wherever needed. Her son had a big heart.

The Old Wise Woman's head drooped as she rocked

back and forth. She was nearly asleep when Paul and Mason returned. "I'd best go and check on family." She pushed to her feet and walked to the door. "I'll be back when sun comes up."

"Thank you, madam," Mason whispered as he gazed down on Abby. Then he walked the seventy-year-old woman to the back porch and helped her down the few steps.

***

Paul reached for Abby's wrist, listened to her pulse and felt her forehead for a sign of fever. "She's doing well, considering she fell so far into that deep hole. She could have broken her neck, along with her arms and legs." Mason agreed as he sat down in the rocker.

"Do you have any idea how long she'll be out like this? Shouldn't we try to wake her?" Mason asked.

"I want some of the swelling to go down on her forehead. She took a blow to the head when she landed on that hard ground. By the way, I hope someone placed a cover over that hole. I would hate for some of the children to fall in it."

"A couple of my men placed large planks over it," Mason replied. "Why don't you go and get a few hours' rest. It'll be morning soon. I'll rest here in that overstuffed chair and watch Abby. And if she wakes up, I'll send a man to get you."

Paul didn't realize he'd been holding Abby's hand the whole time. He placed it down beside her and gave

Mason a nod. "I believe I will do just that." Paul turned and left the room.

## Chapter 20

Early the next morning, Cactus Flower woke Mason out of a deep sleep. She stood next to the stuffed chair, shaking him by his shoulder. He opened his eyes and peered around. "Your woman is moving about and making noise," she said. Mason wiped his eyes as he glanced at the bed and saw that Abby held her head as she tried to sit up.

"Thanks, Cactus Flower. Please start breakfast if you haven't already. I think Abby will be hungry."

"Good morning," Mason spoke softly to Abby as he stooped down beside her. He reached out and gently pressed her shoulders back down on the bed.

***

Abby jerked away from the giant of a man. Her eyes

were wide with fear. She was afraid, but she had no idea why. He had spoken to the scary-looking Indian woman and said for her to cook some food.

"Please don't be afraid. No one here is going to harm you in anyway."

Abby had no idea where she was or who this stranger was who had stooped down beside her bed. Feeling befuddled, she shook her head from side to side to clear her thoughts, which only served to cause pain to race across her forehead.

"Who are you?" Abby asked as tried to scoot her body to the other side of the bed. Her left foot felt heavy and it pained her to move it.

"My name is Mason. Do you remember your name?"

Abby looked hard at Mason and tried to remember her own name. She shook her head slowly, baffled that she couldn't remember. "Why don't I know—me?" Tears brimmed in her eyes before she could control them. "You seem to know me." She frowned at Mason as she wiped her misty eyes.

"I do. I do know you, I mean, but you must stay calm and don't try to force anything to come to you. You have a bump on your forehead, and we hope that with plenty of rest the swelling will go down and you will feel better. Maybe then your memory will come back."

"How did I get hurt?" Abby gingerly touched the bandage that was covering the wound on her forehead.

"You fell down into a deep dark hole out in the woods." Mason lips pressed together in a single line.

A loud knock on the back door got Mason's attention. Abby reached down and pulled the covers up to her shoulders and ducked her chin under them.

***

Cactus Flower was telling Paul that the girl was awake in her room.

"Good morning, Paul," Mason called and waited for him to come down the hall. When he appeared, Mason explained that Abby was awake and asking questions, but she didn't know her own name.

***

Paul hurried past Mason into the room. Abby looked like a terrified rabbit. She was peeking out from under the blue and green quilt.

"Good morning, Miss." Paul had removed his hat and managed a smile. "You have no reason to be scared of me. I'm a doctor. I bandaged the wound on your forehead and wrapped your ankle."

He stared at the young girl's beautiful green eyes. Bella's eyes. He felt his guts twist into knots as he gazed at this lovely girl's face. His instincts told him that this girl was his daughter, his lovely three-year-old baby who was all grown up, and was watching his every move.

"May I look at your foot?" Paul asked after he had cleared his head and gathered his thoughts back to the present.

Lowering the quilt from her chin, she murmured,

"Yes," and attempted to sit up so she could see it, too.

"Please continue to lie still." Mason placed a pillow behind Abby's head so she wasn't lying flat on the bed. She gave him a smile of gratitude.

"Your foot is looking better. Most of the swelling has gone down, but it will still hurt for you to try to stand on it. It will be all shades of black and purple for a while, but that will soon fade. Does it hurt much?" Paul asked.

"No, some yes, but I haven't tried to stand."

"Please don't try to stand. Mason can carry you to the table and put something to prop your foot up on. Are you still having pain across your forehead?"

"Some."

"When you fell, you landed on the right side of your head. This has caused you not to be able to remember. In time, with plenty of rest, your memory will return. It could come back all at once or in bits and pieces. Both are normal."

***

Abby watched Paul as he talked to her. Something about this man made her feel that she knew him, but she couldn't be sure.

"Do you know me, too, like he does?" Abby tilted her head toward Mason.

"No, I'm sorry to say that I don't. I'm a lumberjack who came to Eagle's Nest to help clear some land for Mason. He needs more grazing land for his horses and cattle."

"But, you're a doctor."

"I'm not a practicing doctor anymore, but I was once years ago. Now I'm a lumberjack with a small business that keeps me busy. I'd better go now and put my men to work, but I will check on you tonight. Please eat, get plenty of rest and don't try to force your memory."

Paul turned to Mason and motioned for him to follow him out of the room. "I think she'll be fine. Please have the Old Wise Woman come and sit with her some. You can move her to the kitchen or parlor for a little while. She needs to lie down as much as possible."

"I'll make sure she is never left alone."

***

Mason patted Paul on the back and asked if he would like to stay for breakfast. He declined saying that he had eaten an hour ago and was ready to get to work. Mason watched him as he rode out of the yard toward the pasture.

Once he was gone, Mason turned to Cactus Flower and asked if she would prepare a plate of food for Abby. After pouring him a fresh cup of coffee, she reached for a dish, and piled scrambled eggs, bacon, a biscuit and a small bowl of creamy oatmeal on a tray. Mason carried the food into the bedroom where Abby lay resting.

Abby's eyes widened when she saw the big tray of food. "That smells wonderful. I am hungry," she said. As she pushed herself to a seated position, she asked

Mason, "Am I supposed to remember that I'm hungry?"

He laughed at her question. "I think that is just a survivor instinct."

"Well, I'm glad that I have that survivor whatever, because this biscuit looks wonderful. Did that little Indian woman cook these?" Before Mason could answer her question, Cactus Flower's voice came from the back porch.

"Morning, Cactus Flower," said another voice.

"We have another visitor," Mason said to Abby as he hurried to the kitchen.

"Good morning," Mason said as he led the Old Wise Woman to Abby's bedroom. He made the introductions and said that he was going to leave Abby in her capable hands for a few hours.

As soon as Mason walked out of the room, Abby spoke softly. "Oh, I'm so glad to see another woman. I need to use the water closet something awful. I thought I was going to wet myself, but I couldn't ask that man, Mason, to help me with something so personal."

The Old Wise Woman gave a hearty laugh and instructed her patient on the use of a bedpan until she could place her foot on the floor.

## Chapter 21

Mason rode his horse out to the land that he wanted cleared by Paul and his crew. The lumberjacks were already busy marking several trees that they would take down that day.

He always enjoyed watching the lumberjacks decked out in their colorful work clothes—plaid shirts and knee-length breeches that tied at the knees to hold their pants close to the body. Their bright colorful socks were pulled up to their knees and tucked under the knee-length pants. Wide belts and suspenders that crisscrossed in the back held up the men's pants. All the men wore short, sturdy work boots.

Paul's men were skilled and worked long and hard hours each day to bring down a big tree. Mason was excited each time a fir or a redwood tree would fall exactly where the lumberjack said it would. After a few days of chopping limbs and making a massive pile of branches and brush, the men would start working on the actual tree trunk.

Some trees took as many as three days to bring down, but this land didn't have many giants, as the lumberjacks called them. This section of land had tall slim trees which wouldn't take the men too long to chop down.

Clearing away the stumps would be a long tenuous job that required men to work with sturdy mules to pull them out of the ground. Mason figured that Paul and his crew would be working for him for months.

Mason was happy to know that Paul would be around for some time. He wanted to have excellent doctor's care for Abby while she was recovering from her memory loss. He signaled to Paul as he tied his horse to a tree out of the way of the working men.

"Do you have any special instructions about the clearing of this land, Mason?" Paul asked as his friend walked toward him.

"No, I can't think of anything. You and your men always do a good job. I have something else to take care of. I'm going to the trading post to question those two brothers who tried to kidnap Abby. I was wondering if you would like to tag along and hear what they have to say." Mason scanned his land and shook his head. "Frankly, I don't know what to do with them. The Marshall doesn't come this way often, and Eagle's

Station doesn't have a jail. Some of the men are still riled up and want to hang the brothers, but I'm not much for punishing a man without a trial."

"Let's go and talk with them. After we learn what they had planned to do with your wife, you can decide what to do," Paul said.

As Mason and Paul tied their horses to the hitching rail, small Indian children were playing on the front porch of the trading post. A little boy came charging at Mason, wrapped his arms around his right leg and sat down on his foot.

Mason laughed, bent down and rubbed the boy's coal black hair. "Hang on!" he called as he lifted his leg and started walking the boy back to the porch.

"Paul, this is Little Bear, my friend." The boy continued to sit perched on Mason's boot.

"Fine-looking youngster," Paul replied. "Is he going to roost on your leg the whole time we're here?"

Mason laughed and reached down to the boy. "Up you go."

Little Bear beamed as Mason gave him several pennies. "One for you and one is for your friends. Share with them now, you hear?"

The excited children raced up the steps into the trading post to purchase themselves a piece of candy.

"Smithy!" Mason called to the owner of the livery as they headed to where he was working on a horse's hoof.

"Morning," Smithy said, as he lowered the horse's

leg and gave it a good firm pat. "Ya' come to talk to them fellows that tried to harm your Misses?"

"Yes. I want to be finished with this ugly business."

Mason and Paul followed Smithy to the back of the livery where the two brothers were lying on their bunks.

"Get up, those men are here." Sandy, the youngest brother, jumped up and slapped his brother on the back.

Mason towered over the men. "Stay seated, boys. We're going to have a little chat. I want the truth and nothing else." Mason scowled at one brother, then the other.

The two men didn't respond or offered to begin the conversation.

"Tell me why you were attempting to kidnap my wife?" Mason demanded.

Neither of the men said a word, so Mason continued. "There's a gang of men who are eager to hang you two. If you answer my questions, I might save you from them. Now, I am going to ask you again. Why were you attempting to kidnap my wife?"

***

Sandy couldn't hold his tongue any longer. His brother had threatened to kill him if he said anything that would make matters worse for them.

"Listen, we really didn't mean her any harm. That woman, Lucinda, and that big Black man who worked for her at The Red Dog Saloon made us come here to bring that pretty girl back to her. She lied to us! She said that the girl wanted to come back home—to her."

"Why were you asked to come and get my wife?"

"We didn't know that she was married," Sandy said excitedly. "Well, it's like this. We run up a bar bill and a couple of gaming debts that we couldn't pay. Big Sal, who guards the ladies, said that we would meet up with a bad accident if we didn't cooperate and come and get the girl."

"So, do you owe this Lucinda money or the saloon?" Paul asked.

"The saloon, I guess. Don't she own the place?" Sandy asked.

"No, Lucinda and Big Sal just work there and have for years," Paul said.

***

Mason was surprised that Paul knew so much about The Red Dog Saloon where Abby lived with her mama. "When you asked my wife to go with you, what did she say?" Mason was interested in this answer.

"Well, she said that she didn't know why that woman sent for her, because she was married now and she didn't want to leave her home," Sandy said.

"After she said she didn't want to go with you, what did you do then?" Mason asked.

Willie glanced at Sandy, then Willie finally spoke for the first time. "Well, I grabbed her arm and pulled her to the barn. As I was trying to get a saddle and blanket on a horse, Sandy turned her loose and she ran out of the barn into the woods. Honest man, we didn't hurt her." Willie glanced from Mason to Paul.

"She ran into the woods and we tried to catch her. But she ran and ran. As she was running away from us, she stopped to get her breath, and we caught up to her. Then next thing we knew, she was screaming and she disappeared right in front of our eyes. The earth just opened and swallowed her up. We couldn't believe it. One minute she was there and the next she was gone. We ran over to where she had been standing and looked down into the dark hole in the ground. There, at the bottom of that dark pit, she laid still as death. I shot a snake that was in the pit next to her. The girl didn't even flinch. I was sure she was hurt bad or dead." Willie glanced again at Mason.

"We knew that we couldn't get her out of the hole. We didn't have a long enough rope and neither one of us are strong enough to carry a body and climb out of that hole," Willie said, almost sounding remorseful.

"After you realized that you couldn't get her out, you ran off and left her to die?" Paul said through gritted teeth.

"We didn't want her to die! I was nearly crazy worrying about her. I was scared to death that she had already died from the fall. She was so still." Sandy covered his face with his hands and cried. "I'm sorry, man, really I am, but I was scared of what might happen to us."

"We are truly sorry, but we are very happy that your wife is going to be all right," Willie said. "We might as well go to jail because with that old woman and Big Sal after us, we will be dead men once they catch us."

Mason didn't know how he felt about the two stupid young men. He had to get away from them before he smashed their heads together or strangled them with his bare hands.

***

Paul told Smithy to lock them back up. "Mason will let you know what to do with them in a little while. He wants them gone for sure, one way or the other." Paul made that last remark loud enough for the two boys to hear him. They needed to be scared. He caught up with Mason while he paced in front of the trading post. Mason called Mr. Peterson to come outside and join in the conversation about the two kidnappers.

"Now that you've talked with them, what do you want to do?" Peterson asked.

Mason looked to Paul and said for him to sit down on the steps. His eyes rose to heaven and he said a prayer to God to help him make the right decision about the young men's future.

"This is the way I see it." Mason said, "The two men were desperate and forced to come for Abby. They believed that she wanted to go back to San Francisco, but when she declined, they got scared of what Big Sal and Lucinda would do to them if they returned without her."

Mason looked at the expressions on Paul and

Peterson's faces and continued with his decision. "Honestly, I don't believe that they intended on harming her, but when she ran, they chased her. After she fell in the hole, they were afraid that they had killed her. It is true that they couldn't get her out without coming for help, but it's hard for me to forgive them for leaving her. I might feel better about them if they had come for help."

Paul finally spoke up. "Are you inclined to let them go free? If they return to San Francisco, they will most likely meet up with an unfortunate accident—of course, by the hands of Big Sal or one of his so-called friends."

"I am prepared to let them go. If they have any sense at all, they will head to Texas and get jobs as wranglers. They can ride and they're young enough to get a fresh start somewhere else where no one knows them," Mason said, as he waited for a response from Paul or Mr. Peterson. Neither man said anything.

"I had thought about putting them to work for a while, but I'm afraid that would only stir up trouble among the men. They're already set to string them up."

"Yep, that's a fact. I had to run a few of them off my porch last night. They were all liquored up and ready to have a hanging party," Peterson said as he placed both hands on his trousers and hiked them up.

"Well, it's settled then. I don't want the angry men to do something foolish and say that they were only protecting my wife. I'm going to give those two boys a little stake and fill their saddlebags with grub. I'll send them on their way with the understanding that if they ever come back here, they will be placed under arrest until the marshal shows up."

"If there was any kind of law here now, they would have to face charges. They're fortunate to have a good man like you giving them a second chance in life." Paul stood on the porch steps and dusted the seat of his breeches. "I think you made a good decision, son," he said. "I've got to get back to work."

***

Mason went and got Smithy. They walked to the bunkhouse and laid down the law to the two brothers. "I'm turning you loose with the understanding that you'll not return to Eagle's Station again. If you do, I will personally lock you up until the marshal returns."

The two brothers looked at each other but neither one of them moved from their bunk.

"Grab your belongings and let's head down to the trading post. I'm going to get you some grub and a little money to help you get a new start somewhere else. If I were you, boys, I would head for Texas. There's plenty of work for two strapping young men like yourselves, and plenty of country to get lost in. I certainly would stay away from gambling tables and hard liquor. Do I make myself clear?"

Willie and Sandy jumped off their bunks and dressed as fast as they could. Mason, Mr. Peterson and Smithy watched the two young men ride out of Eagle's Station heading east, straight to Texas.

Mason headed toward his horse and gathered the reins in his hands. "Thank you for your help. I'm glad to get this ugly business settled." The two men gave him a nod and watched as he rode down the trail to his ranch where his young wife was waiting.

## Chapter 22

Abby was sitting at the kitchen table with her foot propped up on a small stool when Mason returned to the ranch. She had a bowl of potatoes sitting in front of her. "What's going on here?" Mason asked as he glanced at Cactus Flower standing in front of the stove.

"We're cooking lunch for the men. Cactus Flower said that I cooked for your ranch hands and now we have the lumberjacks to cook for, too."

"Well, that's right, I guess. Paul's men can cook for themselves, especially while you are recovering," Mason said. It was a fact that his cook, Billy, and Cactus Flower had prepared breakfast and the evening meal for Paul's crew when they worked for him before. Sandwiches and fruit had been packed every morning in their lunch pails for their noon meal.

"There is nothing wrong with my hands, sir. I can't lie around when there's work to be done. I might not remember who I am, but I remember how to peel potatoes and do other things in the kitchen. That's kind of funny, isn't it?" She smiled and turned back to her bowl of spuds.

"My name is Mason. Please do not call me *sir*."

"What is my name?"

Mason gave her a questionable look as if he were trying to decide whether to answer her or not.

"No one has called me anything but madam or miss since I woke up yesterday. I must have a name." Abby asked, looking so pitiful that Mason had to answer her.

"Your name is Abigale Mills Waters. I call you Abby."

***

Abby felt as if she had been hit on the head. Her last name was Waters—just like the stranger's house she was living in. Was she married? Was this man her husband? All of these wild thoughts were flowing through her mind. How come he hadn't told her this from the beginning when she had awakened?

The giant of a man bent down and felt her head. "Abby, are you all right? Paul, the doctor, asked me not to tell you anything, but since you are asking, I feel that you should have an answer."

"Are you—my husband?"

"Yes, but we haven't been married very long." He

looked to where Cactus Flower was standing and bent down beside his wife. "We haven't shared a—uh…a marriage bed as yet." His face looked like it was on fire.

"Why is that? Don't you like me?" Abby asked. Every married couple that she knew slept in the same bed. They even hugged and kissed. This man had hardly touched her, much less acted like a husband to her.

"Of course, I like you. It's just that my uncle sent you here to marry me and we were total strangers. I thought you should have some time to get to know me before we—you know.

"Have we gotten to know each other yet?" she asked.

"I think so," he said with a shy grin, "but now that you are hurt and you can't remember me or much about your own life, I think we should continue like we have been until you have recovered." Mason played with the collar of his shirt and looked anywhere but at her.

Abby sighed and looked a little confused. "I've finished the potatoes, Cactus Flower. I think I'd better go back to my room and rest."

Mason rushed to the chair, placed his arms across her back and lifted her legs. She was as light as a feather, but she felt wonderful in his arms. He carried her to the bedroom and gently placed her on the bed. He helped her adjust her left ankle and covered her with the pretty quilt.

"Thank you—husband," she said as she closed her

eyes.

Mason stood looking down at her. He wiped his hand across her forehead and felt the bump that had formed when she had fallen.

Abby pretended to be asleep as she peeked through her eyelids to watch the handsome man who was her new husband.

***

When Mason returned to the kitchen, Cactus Flower had the potatoes boiling and the big pot of stew set aside to serve when everything else was ready.

"In the morning, I will help you make sandwiches for Paul's crew for lunch. I'm going to tell Billy that he will have to help you prepare dinner. Abby is not well enough to cook for all those men. I will hire someone else to help if needed," he said.

Early the next morning, Mason poured himself a cup of hot coffee and watched as Cactus Flower sliced bread for several dozen sandwiches for the lumberjacks' lunches. He went to the cellar and brought up a big ham. While slicing the ham, Billy arrived and began making biscuits.

"We're almost out of bread. Your woman makes the bread," Cactus Flower said.

Mason looked to the high heavens and sighed. Until Abby got hurt, he didn't realize how much she had done to make this kitchen and his household run so smoothly.

"Well, I will have to go to the trading post and buy

some fresh loaves from Mrs. Peterson when I come in from work." Mason shook his head in disgust while slapping ham between two pieces of bread. "I'll ask Mrs. Peterson if she knows someone who would be willing to come in and help with the baking."

The Old Wise Woman knocked on the back door. "Good morning," Mason said, pleased to see her. "Did you come to help Abby?"

"Yes, is she awake? I will help her wash her hair and do a few other personal things for her.

"That's nice of you. She is trying to stay up too long and not getting enough rest. Please try not to let her become too tired."

"I know White man is a good doctor, but I think she will rest better if she can sit outside in the sunshine and help with the cooking. All the men love her bread and sweets." The Old Wise Woman spun around and hurried down the hall to Abby's room without waiting for a response from Mason.

"Women," murmured Mason, "good thing they aren't in the army. None of them can take orders. They'd be shot for disobeying." Mason gave Cactus Flower a hard stare and headed for the barn.

Billy rang the porch bell, signaling the men to come eat breakfast. The fifteen men filed in quietly and took plates of food from Billy. Some sat at the big kitchen table while others sat at an outside table on the porch. The lumberjacks took the lunch pails and went to the flatbed wagon that would carry them to the pasture to work. One of the men looked in his lunch pail and grunted, "You can shore tell Mrs. Waters didn't prepare our lunch."

***

Abby felt terrific after a tub bath and a shampoo. Her golden curls hung down her back nearly to her tiny waist. "I would like to sit on the porch steps and let the sunshine and wind dry my hair. I'm so tired of being in that bedroom." Abby had a flash of memory of being in a room that felt like a prison because she couldn't go outside. *I wonder if I've been locked away somewhere.*

"You must be careful with your foot, but I think the sunshine will be good medicine. Cactus Flower and I can help you outside," said the Old Wise Woman.

Billy and Cactus Flower were cleaning the kitchen and starting lunch for Mason's ranch hands when Old Wise Woman asked for Cactus Flower's assistance in helping Abby onto the porch. Billy was placing a big pot of pinto beans on the stove and declared he would make chili for lunch.

Then he strolled past Abby as she sat on the porch steps. "Can I get you something before I go to the bunkhouse and get a couple hours of sleep?" Billy asked, his eyes darting past her to the bunkhouse.

"I'm fine, thank you," Abby called behind him as he hurried to take a nap."

"That's one lazy White man," said the Old Wise Woman.

"Really? Why does Mr. Waters—my husband, keep him on?"

"Wonder that myself," she replied with a smile.

"I think I'm ready to go back inside to the kitchen. I can sit at the counter and mix up some cookies and start some fresh bread. I may not remember much, but I can cook and I am bored."

"Your man is not going to be happy. He says rest."

"Yes, I know, but he's not my boss. I want to cook for the men. Cactus Flower has to be tired and I know she needs rest, too."

***

When Mason came into lunch with the men, the house smelled wonderful. There was no hiding the fact that Abby had been cooking, because Billy's food never smelled so good.

A big pot of chili simmered next to pans of fresh cornbread on the stove. Platters of sugar cookies and a gingersnap cake were sitting in the middle of the table. Mason grabbed a cookie and shoved it in his mouth before he started down the hall to see his disobedient wife. He knocked on her door and opened it before she could say come in.

Mason took a seat on the side of Abby's bed. He was so upset that she was doing too much and not following his instructions.

Just as he began to speak, she waylaid him by placing her soft right hand on his face. "Hello, husband," Abby whispered softly to him as she ran her hand over his face. He felt like he was being stroked by an angel. She looked like one too, with her long blonde curls hanging loosely down around her shoulders. Her innocent expression with those big green eyes made him forget his own thoughts.

"Abby, the smell in the house is a dead giveaway that you, young lady, have been doing too much." Mason knew Abby wanted to stay up and help with the cooking and other small household chores. She was trying her best to get him to change his mind and allow her out of bed. He knew Abby wasn't used to lying around, but Paul said he was sure she had a concussion and that was the reason she couldn't remember her past. He took her hand and held it tight, then kissed her fingertips and bolted to his feet.

"Now, you need as much rest as possible. If you will follow orders and rest this afternoon, I will consider allowing you outside on the porch tomorrow."

Abby smiled.

"I know the men will appreciate the cookies and the cake, but I am concerned that you aren't getting enough rest." When she didn't reply, he shook his head and said, "I'd better get to the kitchen before the men eat everything."

Abby wiggled her little finger at him to come closer to her. "I made a cookie jar just for you and it's full," she whispered and gave him a sweet smile.

Mason was pleased at her thoughtfulness. Roberta, Uncle Jackson's housekeeper, had always had a full cookie jar just for him. Mason swallowed the lump in his throat and bent and kissed her on the forehead. He left the room smiling.

***

As Abby lay in the bed after Mason left, she had a flash of memory, t*he feel of soft lips grazing her forehead with a kiss.* Mason had just kissed her, but this was different. There seemed to be a faint wisp of unrecognizable scent in the air. *Could this have been her mama kissing her good night when she was a small child?* "Oh, how I wish I could remember my mama," she said as she turned on her side and cried for the first time since she learned that she'd lost her memory.

## Chapter 23

The next morning when Mason came into the kitchen, he found Abby sitting at the counter making biscuits. The coffee was perking and cinnamons rolls were in the oven.

"Well, Miss Abby, just how long have you been out of bed?" Mason questioned her, irritated that she had been working in the kitchen. He noticed her eyes were puffy, like she had been crying.

"I couldn't sleep since I had such a long nap yesterday. I wanted to make something special for the men. There's enough rolls to place one in each of the lumberjacks' lunch pails."

Cactus Flower poured Mason a cup of coffee. He took the cup and sat at the kitchen table. Billy, the cook, came storming through the back door offering apologies for oversleeping.

Mason gave him a hard stare and decided not to say anything. After draining his coffee cup, Mason rose from the table and said he was going to the barn. "Ring the bell when the food is ready, and Billy, be quick about it. Some of the men have to work around here."

***

Abby cut cold pork roast that was left from last night's dinner and made sandwiches for Paul's men. She placed a fresh cinnamon roll and a few sugar cookies in each lunch pail to go with the sandwiches. After everyone had eaten the hearty breakfast, they left patting their stomachs.

Joey said, "You shore are a good cook, Mrs. Waters." Several more of the men expressed their gratitude for the sweets and happy that she was feeling better.

Billy placed all the plates and silverware in a big pan of hot soapy water. He washed as Abby dried the dishes while Cactus Flower put everything away. Now, it was time to start preparing lunch.

The Old Wise Woman arrived and helped Abby with her morning bath and plaited her long blonde hair.

"You should rest," the Old Wise Woman told Abby.

"I want to sit on the porch and enjoy the morning sun while I read several passages in my Bible. Since I've been hurt, I haven't been able to read. For some reason, I like reading the Bible. Maybe this is something that I did before."

"I will ask the fat little man to come and help me with you," she said.

Abby laughed, thinking that Billy was fat, but she would have never said so. Indians say what they believe, thought Abby.

After Billy helped get Abby settled on the porch, he went down into the cellar to finish preparing deer steaks for supper. For lunch they would serve homemade soup and sandwiches to the ranch hands.

Sitting outside felt wonderful with the morning sun on her face and the fresh breeze in her hair. As Abby flipped the pages through her Bible, she heard giggling. She glanced up from the book and peered around. At the edge of the yard, behind a tree, something moved, followed by another giggle, this time louder.

"Come out, come out, whoever you are. I see you." Abby called almost like she was singing to the children. Since Abby had been at Eagle's Station, she had not seen any children, White or Indians. In San Francisco, she hadn't been around small children since she'd left school at the age of fourteen.

Slowly, a little girl stepped out from behind a tree. Abby's mouth was agape. She thought the child was the most beautiful little girl she had ever seen, even if her hair was messy and her Indian dress dirty and too big.

"Come closer." Abby held both hands out signaling the child to come to her.

The girl stared at Abby, but refused to budge. Then she disappeared behind the tree.

Abby shoulder sagged. She was disappointed that the child had gone. "Please come back," she called. Abby eased to the edge of the seat on her chair. How she wished she could walk so she could go in the woods to find her.

Voices rang out in Indian language behind the big tree. Finally the girl reappeared with an Indian boy that could have been her twin. Both children stood as still as statues and stared. She could tell they were intrigued but afraid to come closer.

Abby smiled at the children. They stared back at her without any expression on their dirty faces.

"Cactus Flower," Abby called. She wanted the old Indian woman to tell the children to come and sit with her on the porch. When Cactus Flower saw the children, she shooed them away like they were pesky animals.

"Stop, please," Abby scolded. "Don't scare them away. Please call to them and tell them to come and sit with me. Bring a plate of sugar cookies."

"You feed them and they will never leave you alone," Cactus Flower muttered.

"Hurry, I don't want them to be afraid of me and run off. I like children." Abby smiled to herself. *There's one more thing I remember about myself. Maybe I was a school teacher.*

Once Cactus Flower gave Abby the plate of cookies, she spun around and went back in the house. The children's eyes were as big as saucers when they eyed the treat.

Abby held the plate out to them and motioned for them to come and get one. She picked a cookie off the plate and began eating. The two children took a step toward her and then another. It was only a minute before they were standing directly in front of her. The little girl looked at Abby's foot and said in perfect English, "Hurt?"

Abby smiled and replied, "Yes."

"Where are your sticks?" the boy asked.

"Sticks? Oh, you mean crutches." Abby laughed. "I don't have any, but I can hop on one foot to move around." She smiled—the boy's English was perfect, too.

The boy reached for another cookie and said thank you as he stuffed it in his mouth. Abby grinned at him and offered the girl another one.

Curious about the children, she asked, "Where do you live and who takes care of you?"

"Our *Co-shi*," said the little girl. "We live in her cabin with Running Deer."

From the kitchen, Cactus Flower said, "They live with the Old Wise Woman and they call her *Co-shi*, which means *grandmother* in English.

"You speak good English," Abby said to the little girl.

"You speak pretty, too," she replied. Before Abby realized it, the small girl was standing between her legs and pressing against her. Abby reached down and picked her up and placed her on her lap so she wouldn't step on her bad foot. She smelled fishy, but Abby didn't care. She had never been this close to a small child before. *How did I know that?*

The little girl shifted to face Abby and pulled on the necklace that held her locket. "What's this?"

"It's a special necklace that has pictures in it."

"See? Please."

Abby opened the locket and looked at the two people. She studied the woman in the picture more closely and saw the resemblance. *This has to be my mama,* Abby thought. The man was handsome. There was something familiar about him.

"You?" the child asked, as she reached her hand to touch Abby's blonde curls.

"No. It's my mama." A momentary vision of her mother appeared in her mind. Her beautiful mama had golden hair and lovely green eyes. Abby didn't know if she wanted to shout with joy or cry. She knew her mama was dead.

Abby wiped her eyes as she continued to watch the little boy who sat on the edge of the porch. He was quiet and only talked when spoken to.

"What do I call you?" Abby asked the children.

"My name is Little Bear and her name is *Sehoy*. It means beauty, so we call her Beauty."

"A lovely name for a beautiful child," Abby said to the little girl, who smiled. "So Little Bear and Beauty, do you go to school?"

"No school." Little Bear explained. "Our *Co-shi* teaches us letters and numbers."

"Are there other children in the village?"

"Yep, but I'm the strongest and fastest." Little Bear said as he puffed out his tan chest.

He looked straight at Abby and spoke like a grown man. "What do we call you?"

"Miss Abby. Can you say that?"

"Miss Ab-by. I like that. Beauty can say that too."

"I bet Beauty is the prettiest girl child in the village." Abby said as she squeezed the child in her arms. Beauty giggled and wiggled until Abby stood her on her own bare feet.

"I got to wet," she exclaimed and jumped off the porch and ran into the woods.

In just a few minutes, the Old Wise Woman emerged from the trees holding Beauty's hand. "Come, Little Bear, it's time to go home. You should not bother Mrs. Waters."

"Her name is Miss Ab-by."

The Old Wise Woman raised her eyebrows and peered at Abby.

"Please, the children are great company. Let them come and see me whenever they wish." Abby looked at the children with a sweet smile.

"Come tomorrow," Little Bear said, hurried to his grandmother's side and took her other hand. Abby watched them disappear and walk into the woods.

Sitting all alone on the porch, Abby took the

necklace from around her neck and studied the two pictures again. Her dear mama was so lovely. She held the locket next to her heart and let the tears flow freely. A flash of remembrance came to her so clearly. *Her Mama was telling her to leave her home,* but she had no idea why.

# Chapter 24

After several weeks, Abby's dark bruises faded away and she was able to walk on her left foot. She was having many flashbacks of memory, but she didn't tell Mason, her patient husband. She still didn't remember much about San Francisco or how she came to be at Mason's ranch, much less being a young married woman. Mason's and Abby's life had evolved into a daily routine.

Paul Miller and his lumberjacks were still cutting down trees, burning branches and leaves in the pasture, so Abby and Cactus Flower prepared breakfast and dinner for them along with Mason's ranch hands. Abby enjoyed packing the lumberjacks' lunch pails each morning so they could have a nice mid-day meal in the woods. She prepared a light lunch for Mason and his ranch hands each day as well.

With so many more men working on the ranch, Cactus Flower had chosen another Indian girl to come in and help with the wash twice a week and clean the house. The weekends were quiet around the ranch as the men fended for themselves or ate in the bunkhouse with Billy, the cook.

Abby enjoyed having the extra help, but she worked as hard as anyone on the place. Buster helped her with her small garden and Mrs. Peterson taught her how to put up vegetables in glass canning jars. Abby and the two Indian children picked wild strawberries and blackberries. Cactus Flower helped her make jam with the berries. Abby giggled with delight when Mason rolled in a barrel of sugar and placed it in the cellar.

Saturday mornings were always exciting to Abby. Mason escorted her to the village where many White and Indian families came down out of the hills and backwoods to shop or swap their wares for needed supplies. It was nice to see other ladies. Abby was lonely and hoped that in time she would become friends with some of the younger women. At times she tried hard to remember someone who might have been her friend back in San Francisco, but no one came to mind.

In the evening, Mason sat in front of the fireplace in their lovely, decorated parlor and read. She joined him after the dinner dishes were washed, dried and put away. It was pleasant to sit and watch Mason read his Bible. Sometimes, she would think about her past and she would ask Mason questions.

"Mason, you told me that you lived in San Francisco as a young man. Did you know me before I came here?"

"Let's see." He hesitated and she could tell he was choosing his words.

"I can't say I knew you well, but I knew your name. In school, you were the little girl who sat under a tree all alone and I was the tall, smart, good-looking young boy who wondered why you didn't play with the other kids," he said, and she could tell he was teasing her.

"Why was I alone and not playing with the other children?"

"As I said, I didn't know you so I'm not sure." He answered.

***

Abby sat with her eyes shut as she rocked softly. He sighed and thought how much he wanted this young woman to come to him as his wife. Sure he could demand his husband rights, but he would never do that. He wanted her to come to him because she loved him.

"Mason, I want to ask you another question. Will you please tell me the truth?"

"Yes, my sweet wife. I will always be truthful with you."

"Paul Miller, who is he? I mean, how well do you know him?"

"Why do you want to know about him?"

"Well, every time he's around me, I have a funny

feeling. It's like I know him—have known him from my past," she said with a deep sigh.

"I see. Well, I met him when I first moved here. I needed some of my land cleared and Mr. Peterson said that Paul was a good man with a small crew of lumberjacks. When you got hurt, he confessed to me that he was a doctor, but he hasn't practiced in years. I was surprised to learn that about him."

"You don't know anything about his past, like when he was a young man?"

"No, he has never talked about himself and I have never thought to ask. Is there a reason you have an interest in him?"

"No, not really. Like I said before, I get a funny feeling when I'm near him," she smiled at Mason and stood. "Well, I think I'd better turn in. Tomorrow will be here soon. Goodnight." Abby stretched and yawned. "Goodness, I must be tired."

As Abby walked past Mason, he reached out and grabbed her hand. She froze and waited. He looked at her hand, turned it over and kissed the inside of her palm. "Goodnight."

***

A tingling sensation rushed through Abby's body as she held her palm close to her heart while walking to her room. She had hoped that he was going to say something to her—but what did she want him to say?

As Abby prepared for bed, she always felt guilty for taking Mason's room and his big four-poster bed that he said he had ordered special because of his size. He couldn't be comfortable on that single bed in the guest room. She suggested to him that they should exchange places, but his only response was "in time."

Once settled in bed, she reached for the locket that her mama had always worn around her neck and opened it. In the dim light of the room, she held the two portraits near the lantern. Tears sprang to her eyes as she gazed at her lovely mama. She wished she was here with her now.

Leaning forward to examine the picture of her papa, she couldn't believe how much the man looked like a younger version of Paul Miller. Could it be possible that this man, a doctor and lumberjack, was her father? If he was her father, why hadn't he said something? Surely he would be happy to see her, wouldn't he? She needed to ask him some questions and show him this picture in the locket.

Early the next morning, after Paul's crew and Mason's ranch hands were gone to work, the house was quiet again. Billy, Cactus Flower and Abby sat at the table having coffee. Billy suggested that they cook a big pot of soup and cornbread for lunch and he would prepare two large slabs of pork chops for the evening meal. "You can cook vegetables to go with the chops and something sweet," he said.

"That's fine," replied Abby. "I'll prepare the cornbread and make four apple pies for dinner. I can also make some spice cake for lunch and cinnamon rolls for Paul's men. They love them in their lunch pails."

Billy got busy preparing the meat and vegetables for the soup and Cactus Flower gathered the ranch hands' dirty laundry to wash. With the rain, washing would have to wait until the sun came out.

Abby was busy making pie crusts when Little Bear came in letting the door slam behind him. He was soaking wet and out of breath from running as fast as his short legs would take him.

"Little Bear, why have you been running and playing out in the rain? You're soaked to the skin and you smell as bad as a wet dog, too."

Abby grabbed a towel from the back porch and wiped his black hair dry. "Is something chasing you?" Abby glanced down at him as she dried his back and shoulders.

***

The child was trying hard to catch his breath as he peered up at Abby. He had raced from the trading post with the first raindrops riveting his face as he ran down the path that led to Mason's ranch. Cutting across the cornfield, pushing away stalks that were taller than he, and stomping away the line of high brush on his right, he continued to run as the rain slashed his body. When he reached the pasture closest to the house, he struggled to open a gate. Giving up on the gate, he finally climbed over and rushed into the back door.

"A big . . . covered wagon  . . . is at the trading post. A big Black man wants you!" Little Bear said, struggling to catch his breath.

"What? Start again, slower this time." Abby hugged the child to her.

"A big man, black as night, is at the trading post. He wants you."

"Me? Why would a man like that want me?" she asked Little Bear.

He lifted his shoulders up and down. "He's scary and big. There's a bad woman with him. You'd better hide."

"I don't remember anyone like that... I don't think. Are the man and woman still at the trading post?"

"They coming here! That's why I ran like a deer to get here and warn you. Old man on porch told man where you live."

"Little Bear, settle down and take a deep breath. I need you to go out to the pasture and get Mason." She placed a jacket over his head and shoulders. "Tell Mason I need him, please."

"I must stay—protect you!" he said as he reached to remove the jacket and pulled out his pocketknife.

***

Abby's eyes opened wide as she looked at Little Bear with a sharp blade in his small hands. He looked grim and angry.

"Please, put that knife away. Go now and get Mason. He will come and protect us." She put the jacket over his head and turned him toward the door. "Watch for

217

Mason since it's raining and he'll most likely be heading home."

"Cactus Flower!" Abby called as she ran out to the wash shed. "Please come in the house. We're going to have some strange company and I'm not sure who they are."

"Don't be afraid. I have my blade if you don't want them here," she responded as she patted her side.

"Thank you, but I'm going to get Billy to be prepared."

Abby opened the cellar door and called down to Billy. He came to the opening and glanced up at her.

"Here I am. What's all that hollering about? What do you need?" he asked.

"Come up here and go get your shotgun. Little Bear says some strangers are coming here and I'm not sure if they are friendly."

"Coming, Madam." Billy tossed his ax down and hurried up the stairs. When he returned to the house and asked Abby who was coming, his white apron was covered with bloody bits of raw meat and his hair was wet from the downpour of cold rainwater.

"Little Bear said he heard a big man—a stranger— asking for me at the trading post. I don't think I know anyone like that" she said, placing her hands on her temples. "He said he's driving a covered wagon and there's a bad woman with him. I sent Little Bear after Mason." Abby handed Billy a clean towel to dry his hair and face.

"Don't you fret. I have this cannon and it will scare the devil out of them." Billy patted his big double-barreled shotgun like he was petting an animal. He took the towel and wiped down the barrel of the gun.

"They could be friends, someone I knew from my past. My memory hasn't returned so I guess we'll have to wait until they get here." Abby poured Billy a cup of hot coffee and offered Cactus Flower a cup, which she refused.

As Abby went back to preparing her pie crusts, she surveyed the kitchen. Billie sat down at the table on the porch for the arrival of the strangers. Abby smiled to herself. She may not remember her past, but she bet she didn't have this much protection in her prior life. Running to get help was one small Indian boy who had the spirit of a grown man, an old woman who would stare down the devil if he came near, and an older man who would blast anyone with his big, double-barreled shotgun if they tried to harm any of them.

Abby washed her hands and placed the apples in the pie crusts as she continued to listen for Mason's return. She set the pies in the oven and sat at the kitchen table next to Cactus Flower.

When lunchtime arrived, the ranch hands washed up and took their places in the kitchen for the mid-day meal. Abby felt safer now that the men were gathered in her kitchen. Mason and Little Bear had not returned to the house and the expected visitors hadn't made an appearance either. Buster said that Mason had left earlier and gone to the trading post for more nails, but he hadn't returned to the pasture.

"There was some gunfire earlier, but we figured some of the local Indians were deer hunting," Mick, Mason's foreman said. "We should get on back to work, but with the rain, we'll wait it out in the bunkhouse. We'll be repairing some fence close to the ranch house when the rain lets up. Ring the bell if you need us."

Abby walked the men to the door and said that she would see them at supper.

## Chapter 25

As Abby, Billy and Cactus Flower sat quietly at the table, the sounds of wagon wheels rattling and mules snorting broke the silence. Billy jumped up and strode to the screen door on the porch. Sitting high on the wagon's bench sat an older woman with wet hair plastered to her head and rain streaming down her shoulders. Her soaked bonnet sat drooping on her head. A huge Black man, damp and dirty, sat next to her. Many colorful arrows stuck out of the white canvas that covered the wagon.

"Well, get down and knock on the door before we drown sitting out here. I ain't got all day." The old woman practically shoved the man off the bench.

Billy stepped out on the porch steps with his double-barreled shotgun lying across his arms and watched the couple. "How can I help you folks?" He said, pointing the gun at the man's chest.

"Hey mister, you don't need that gun. We ain't bringing you no trouble." The man held both hands in the air as he looked down the barrel of Billy's shotgun.

"Well, we'll have to wait and see about that, won't we?" The rain had subsided to a drizzle and the sun was attempting to shine.

"Look, old man, we've had enough trouble like it is. Thank the Lord Mr. Waters came along and chased the wild Indians away. They had us surrounded, and we figured we were dead people for sure."

"Sal, come and help me down from this rolling bucket!" The woman, Lucinda, shouted even though she was only a few feet away.

***

The minute he returned from the trading post, Mason came out of the barn, saw the wagon, and helped the old woman down from the high bench. She had dirt on her face and she smelled musty. The rain had soaked her to the skin.

"Hey man," Mason said to the big man accompanying her, "start unhitching those mules and take them to the barn. There are a few empty stalls and dry rags for you to rub them down. Don't give them any water until they're settled down." Mason offered his hand to help the woman onto the porch.

"You stay here and I'll get some fresh water and dry

towels. I know you will want to get out of those wet things, but first wash your face and hands and remove those wet shoes."

"Don't be giving me orders, young man. I want to go into the house, sit down and have a shot of whiskey to drink." Lucinda tried to scurry around Mason but he held her arm tight.

"This is my home, Madam, and you will do as I say or you can get back on that wagon and take yourself away from here. You aren't an invited guest, and I don't serve hard liquor."

"Forgive me, but I have been half scared out of my wits, I'm soaked to the skin, tired and hungry and I want to see my girl!" she screamed as she began to cry.

"Mason," Abby called to him. "What's going on out here, and who are these people?"

Mason watched Abby's face as the old woman spoke to her. He wanted the old woman to shut her ugly mouth. He had listened to her fuss and grumble for the last mile but she was from San Francisco. She might be able to help Abby because she was the woman who had sent the two young men here to bring her home. He could see in Abby's expression and deep frown that some of the old memories might be forming in her mind.

Lucinda wiped her eyes with the back of her dirty hand and peeked around Mason. "Abigale, my Abby, don't you know me? Surely, you ain't been gone from the saloon that long you would have forgotten your second mama.”

***

Abby approached the old woman, memories swirling around in her head. That voice, she had heard that voice before. But where, who? Slowly she studied the woman who seemed familiar. *Was she familiar because Little Bear had described her this morning, but the sound of her voice, she was sure she knew the voice.*

Abby remembered that voice. Reaching for the door, she could feel her legs go weak as everything that she had forgotten came back into her mind like an enormous tidal wave. *Her mama was dead. She had buried her. A saloon had been her home. Loneliness, an unhappy childhood. Most of all she remembered that woman, Lucinda.*

Abby pivoted away from the voice of her past and stepped back onto the porch steps when total blackness overtook her body and she fell at Billy's feet.

***

“Gosh almighty, Mason, help me get your gal on her bed. Cactus Flower! Bring some water and a few wet rags.” Billy took charge as Mason had trouble moving.

Mason pulled himself together, picked Abby up from the steps and cuddled her in his arms, whispering sweet words as he carried her to bed. Abby's face was as white as a sheet, like she had seen a ghost. *Maybe she had. A ghost from her past. Someone she didn't wish to see ever again.*

Loud footsteps came from the hall, then the woman named Lucinda entered the bedroom and shoved him out of the way.

"I'll care for her," she demanded, attempting to push Mason out of the room.

Mason gripped the woman's elbow, shoved her out of the room and slammed the door in her face. When she reopened the door to gain entrance, Mason gave her a look that dared her to enter.

After Mason was sure that Abby's old caretaker was out of his way, he wiped Abby's face and arms with a cold wet cloth. He kissed her forehead and pleaded with her to wake up. As he continued stroking her face with the soft damp cloth, Abby's eyelids fluttered.

"Abby, sweetheart, it's me, Mason. Please, please open your eyes. I'm here and I will never let anyone hurt you. You're safe with me," he said, just above a whisper.

Loud voices were coming from the kitchen. Mason got up to open the door an inch. Lucinda was telling Billy that she should be the one that fainted. "With all those wild Indians chasing…"

Mason couldn't help but smile as he remembered how he came upon the old woman's covered wagon, driven by a giant of a man and being pulled by four sturdy mules. It had been hard seeing them because the rain was pouring down. He had to get off the trail or be run over by the speeding wagon that was being chased by a band of wild Indians. The man was using his bullwhip on the mules' backs while the woman was screaming at the top of her lungs.

Even with the rain nearly blinding him, he recognized the Indians as the young boys who lived in the hills behind the trading post. The leaders of the group were Little Bear and Running Deer. The other Indians were a little taller than Little Bear and they were shooting their bow and arrows at the white canvas that covered the wagon.

When he caught up with the wagon and was able to stop the mules, he signaled the Indians to retreat and get out of sight before the man started shooting at them with his shotgun.

Mason had not gotten to the bottom of all the trouble as yet, but he would as soon as he had taken care of his wife. He felt sure it had something to do with Abby, because Little Bear had come every day to the house to be with his new friend. He had told the Old Wise Woman that Miss Abby was his future woman and after many moons, he would take her to be his wife.

***

In the kitchen, Lucinda and her companion were retelling the story of the Indian raid on their wagon. The old woman was still shaken and was nearly screaming as she was sure they were going to be scalped or laid out on an ant bed to die.

Billy and Cactus Flower sat at the table and listened in amazement. Billy wanted to laugh but he kept a straight face at the two strangers who seemed to know Abby. For the life of him, he couldn't figure out who the Indians were, because there weren't many of them in the area and the ones that were here were old gentle creatures. There wasn't an Indian for miles that would do harm to anyone.

***

Abby opened her eyes and glanced around the room while attempting to sit up. Mason placed his hand on her shoulder and told her to take it easy.

"You fainted, sweetheart, but you are all right otherwise."

Abby didn't say anything. She laid her head back down on the pillow and watched Mason. He was a handsome man with a sweet smile that touched her soul whenever he looked at her.

Her mind was filled with memories. Mason's Uncle Jackson had sent her to Mason to be his bride. She remembered getting married at the trading post but there'd been no honeymoon. *He thought I was a working girl in the saloon, my home.* The old woman in the kitchen was Lucinda, who had taken care of her while her mama slept during the day and worked at night. Lucinda was responsible for keeping the upstairs clean and meals prepared for the other ladies who worked in the saloon. *Why had Lucinda sent the two young men after her when she knew that she was leaving San Francisco?*

"Abby, can I help you? I feel that some of your

memory has returned. Am I right?"

Abby peered into Mason's eyes and gave him a weak smile. "I haven't been here long but you seem to know how I'm feeling, and now you can almost read my thoughts. How is that?"

"How do I know what you're thinking? I wouldn't say I do, but I can tell when you aren't yourself. I see it in your eyes that you are confused. I want to help you any way I can," he said as he pushed a few blonde curls away from her face.

In barely a whisper, Abby asked Mason the question that was confusing her. "What reason has she given for coming here?"

"I haven't had a chance to question her or the driver, but I think that she has come to take you back to San Francisco."

"Do you want me to return with them, leave here and give you your freedom?"

"Why would you ask that? You're my wife! But to answer your question, I do not wish for you to leave me or your new home."

"This is a lovely place. I love it here." The tension in her head was giving her a terrific headache. "The wide open spaces, my garden, the animals and my new friends mean everything to me. If you wanted me to leave, I believe it would break my heart." She used the edge of the sheet to wipe her eyes.

"Abby, please, this is your home. You never have to leave."

She could tell he had more to say, but his eyes went to the open door.

***

"I'll be back. I'm going to question that old woman and see why she traveled here and how long she plans to stay. You should continue to rest," he said. Leaning down and giving her a kiss on her mouth, he felt her soft sweet lips, and he didn't want to stop with just a kiss, but he forced himself to push away.

## Chapter 26

Mason marched back into the kitchen. He looked at Lucinda and Sal, the driver of her wagon. They both had changed clothes and made themselves presentable. Billy had served everyone lunch. Lucinda and Sal were sitting at the table drinking coffee as Cactus Flower washed the dishes.

Mason sat at the table across from Lucinda and stared at her for a long minute before he finally spoke. The old woman averted her eyes and played with the strap of her handbag.

"All right, Miss Lucinda, what are you doing here? Abby told you before she left San Francisco that she wasn't planning on returning there."

"Mr. Waters, you must understand how much I miss Abby. I watched after her ever since she was a small thing. After her poor mama died, she left the saloon and went to take care of some unknown business. I would have never let her go off on her own. Well, the child didn't come back!" She screamed and held out her hands. "I was beside myself. I sent big Sal out looking for her, but he came back and said he couldn't find her anywhere. You looked everywhere, didn't you, Sal?" She pushed on his shoulder and he shook his head yes.

"Later that day, a tall man dressed like a gentleman's footman came demanding Abby's personal effects and some of Bella's things, too. He had a list prepared by Abby's own hand. I almost had Sal toss him out on his backside, but he threatened me. Said he would get the law to retrieve the things if I didn't get them for him. I pleaded and begged him to tell me where my sweet Abby was, but the old goat just stood glaring down at me and wouldn't tell me anything."

She held her head down and pretended to cry. "I didn't see Abby until the next day at Bella's funeral. She told me she was going away and thanked me for taking care of her. She *thanked* me? I couldn't believe that all she did was say 'thank you' after all the years of me caring for her. She owed me, Mr. Waters, she owed me!"

"What kind of payment were you expecting from a young girl who had just lost her mama?" Mason asked.

"Well, she could have continued working at the saloon. I can tell you now, any number of customers would pay a lot just to spend an hour with that lass, as beautiful as she is."

"How long do you think she would have to work for you to work off her debt: a week, a month, or until her looks faded and she began to look like your other soiled doves?"

She shrugged. "Well, I don't rightly know. Sal and I are moving on to a bigger city and Abby will be the main attraction until we can get a few others to work for us. You see, the saloon in San Francisco wasn't in the best shape after the fire. But with Abby, we can have a traveling saloon and make plenty of money at campsites and a few military posts."

"Lucinda, you are out of your mind if you think Abby will be going anywhere with you. She is my wife. She will not be working for you tomorrow or any other time. Do I make myself clear?" Mason narrowed his eyes and spoke venom with each word.

"Since it is almost dark, you may stay, but I expect you to leave in the morning. My wife has had a shock, which has helped her to regain her memory," Mason said. He noticed Cactus Flower's and Billie's smiles when they heard that Abby's memory had returned.

"We can't leave with all those Indians on the warpath." Lucinda's loud shout made Billy and Cactus Flower both jump. "We need protection or be assured that those heathens have left the area."

"Be assured, madam. They're gone, and you will be too at first light. Now Sal, you'd better go and check over your wagon and mules. I don't care where you go tomorrow, but you will leave. Do you understand me?"

The man pushed away from the table and went out the back door toward his wagon. Mason stood on the back porch and finally stepped outside, walking toward the barn. He needed fresh air because he felt as if he would empty his stomach right in the middle of the yard.

The old bat had just confirmed that his wife had worked in the saloon, entertaining customers. He had already made up his mind that this wasn't true. But now he had to face the truth. He needed to be alone and have time to work things out. He loved her, but how much? His head pounded from the realization of all he had just heard.

"We're here, oh boy!" Mason heard a loud, rough voice coming from the front yard. *Good gracious, who else is going to show up here?*

"Mason! Are you home?" a jolly voice called out.

Mason listened for a fraction of a second. He knew that voice, and it had to be the one person he loved the most in this world. Hurrying out of the barn, he saw his incredible Uncle Jackson standing tall in the front of a covered wagon.

"Here I am, Uncle Jack. Gosh, I can't believe you're here," he exclaimed as he looked up at the distinguished, old man.

"I couldn't stay away another minute, and look who I have brought along." Roberta peeked out from her old-fashion bonnet and grinned.

"Hello, Mason," she said.

"Oh my goodness. This is a wonderful surprise. Abby will be thrilled to see you again, Miss Roberta."

Uncle Jackson jumped to the ground and offered his hand to Roberta. The first thing she did was reach for Mason and give him a big hug as Jackson patted Mason's back.

"Mason, before we go any further, I have an announcement. Miss Roberta is now Mrs. Jackson Waters, your new aunt. We married several weeks ago while we were planning this trip. Can't say this has been a great honeymoon, but I will make it up to her," he said as he glanced at his new bride.

"I'm so happy for the both of you. I always thought of you as family, and now you are my aunt," Mason said as he gave her another hug. "But tell me, why didn't you write and let me know you were coming?"

"The mail service is terrible, so we decided to come and take our chances that you would welcome an uninvited visit from us."

"Come on in the house. Oh, wait. We have two visitors that weren't invited, but they are leaving at first light—one way or the other."

"Mercy, who is here?" Uncle Jackson asked.

"Lucinda and a man called Sal who worked at The Red Dog Saloon in San Francisco." Mason had disgust in his voice.

"Well, well, this is interesting. Do you have a sheriff or marshal nearby? Those two are wanted by the law for stealing from the saloon. I wonder why they made a stop here."

"It seems that they came by to get Abby to go with them to help set up their traveling business, but they got a surprise. My Abby isn't going anywhere with that trash."

Uncle Jackson raised an eyebrow at Mason referring to Abby as his. Jackson led the way into the house like a general. Lucinda, Sal, and Cactus Flower all jumped to attention.

"Well, isn't this a big surprise." Jackson circled the table and gave Lucinda and Sal a stern look. "I never thought to ever see you two again with the law so close on your heels."

"What are talking about, old man?" Lucinda turned as white as a sheet as she held onto the table. "Ain't no law after us because we ain't done nothing?  I never took any money that wasn't mine for the taking."

"Now isn't that interesting? No one said anything about anyone stealing money. But it is a known fact that the safe in the saloon was broken into and all the money was taken. Henry said at least two thousand dollars was stolen."

"That's a lie. Henry is a big fat liar for sure. Wasn't but a few hundred in that . . ." Lucinda stopped mid-sentence.

***

As everyone looked on, Lucinda and Sal inched toward the back door. At that moment, Abby walked into the kitchen. She had heard loud voices that sounded like quarreling. As she entered the room, she focused on Mr. Waters and Roberta. The surprise visitors were almost too much, so she eased down into a chair at the table.

"My goodness, this is a wonderful surprise. Roberta, when did you get here?"

"Oh, honey," Roberta said as she pulled out a chair and sat next to Abby. "We've just arrived. How are you? Have you been sick? You're so pale."

"I had to go line down for a while, but I am better, thank you." Abby glanced at Mason as he moved to stand behind her.

"Let's get you settled and have some refreshments. You both have to be tired after your long trip here," Mason said, interrupting Roberta before she had a chance to quiz Abby more about her health.

***

"The trip wasn't bad," Jackson said, as he watched Lucinda and Sal ease out the door. "Took the train almost all the way. We got the covered wagon in a small town called Cloverleaf, about thirty miles from here. It was a spot in the tracks where the train stops and takes on water."

"You mean to tell me that the train tracks have been completed? I was told that if it ever got built, it would be years from now." Mason shook his head in disbelief.

"If you had been able to receive mail, you would have read about it. Now we can ship supplies to you so much quicker, and you'll get news." Uncle Jackson peered out the window. "By the way, your 'guests' are leaving. I guess there's no need turning them in, seeing as you don't have a sheriff in these parts."

Cactus Flower poured everyone coffee and set a big platter of sugar cookies in the middle of the table. She walked back to the counter and began peeling potatoes.

***

Abby glanced out the window. The sun was going down and the men would be coming in to have their evening meal. She stood and walked over to the counter. "Roberta, please forgive me, but I must help prepare supper for the men. They will be in soon. We've had so much excitement that I haven't even started anything for them to eat."

"Mason, please show me where I can wash and change my traveling clothes. I want to help Abby and Cactus Flower with supper," Roberta said as she jumped up from the table. "Jackson, help Mason bring our things inside and please be quick about it."

"Cactus Flower, please cut those potatoes really small, and we'll fry them like we do for breakfast. We can make biscuits, scrambled eggs, fried ham and bacon to go along with the potatoes and I will open a couple jars of peaches and wild strawberry jam. Billy can make several pots of steaming coffee. I have leftover cinnamons rolls that we can warm in the oven after the biscuits are cooked."

"Abby, it sounds like you are going to feed an army," laughed Roberta.

"They are hardworking men, and they're starving by supper time. We'll have fifteen men to feed, not counting all of us to serve. I don't allow my men to go away from my table hungry."

Roberta smiled at Abby's reference to the ranch hands and the lumberjacks as her men. "I haven't been here long, but it's easy to see that you're happy here, girl."

## Chapter 27

Mason and Uncle Jackson strode outside to the covered wagon where Lucinda and Sal were preparing to leave. Mason placed his boot on one of the spokes of a wheel and cleared his throat before speaking.

"You two can spend the night here and be on your way at first light. I had no idea that you were thieves or I wouldn't have allowed you near my property. But mark this down. I am grateful that once Abby heard your voice, it snapped her memory back. She had already had a few flashbacks, but seeing you helped to completely restore her memory. It was your fault that she got hurt in the first place."

"Mason, may I speak to these two?" Jackson asked, and Mason nodded his assent as his uncle glared at the old woman and her partner.

"I want so bad to put you two behind bars. But, I know over the years that you, Lucinda, did care for Abby and helped Bella. For that I am thankful. You stole from old Henry, but he's a lot better off without you in his saloon. I wouldn't plan on ever returning to San Francisco if I was either of you. As Mason said, don't ever come near Abby again."

Lucinda cringed at Uncle Jackson's threatening tone and only managed to sputter a stream of incoherent words in response. Jackson turned on his heel and strode back to the house.

***

All the men gathered into the kitchen. Each one removed their boots and hats before entering the room filled with the aroma of sweet rolls and bacon. They waited until Mason signaled for them to take their places. Before the blessing was said, Mason introduced his uncle and aunt. The men smiled and began passing the food once Mason completed a long blessing. They were all thrilled to hear that Abby's memory had returned and she was doing well.

Paul walked over to Abby and asked how she felt since her memory had returned. She gave him a reassuring smile and told him to sit and eat before the men devoured all the food. He laughed and took his seat next to Mason.

Paul smiled at his men as they joked about several events of the day, but he noticed how Mr. Waters kept his eyes on him. Paul knew Mason's uncle from the past. He remembered that he owned a sawmill a few miles from town and his young nephew had come to live with him. Paul was sure that Jackson Waters recognized him, and he knew that the older man was curious.

When supper was completed and the men had taken their leave, Paul thanked the ladies for a good meal and asked to speak with Abby alone. Mason nodded, then the two walked into the parlor.

***

"Why does the big lumberjack wish to speak with Abby and not with you too?" Uncle Jackson asked Mason.

Mason poured his uncle and aunt another cup of coffee and relayed the story about how Lucinda's hired men came to the ranch to take Abby back to San Francisco. He told of how the men chased her and how she had fallen and lost her memory.

"Paul Miller wasn't always a lumberjack. When Abby was hurt from her fall, Paul confided in me that he was a doctor. I was surprised but pleased. He took excellent care of her. Now that her memory has returned, he is probably talking to her about what she remembers."

"Does she know that Paul Miller is her father?" Jackson said.

"What?" Mason and Roberta asked at the same time.

"I knew him when he was a young doctor, married to

Bella. He was a well-respected doctor who worked from sunup to sundown."

Mason signaled to his uncle to be quiet as Abby and Paul came back into the kitchen.

"I want to bid all of you a good evening as I have to be up before the sun in the morning." Paul said, as he smiled again at Abby.

"See you at breakfast," Mason said.

***

Abby headed to the bedrooms. Mason had only prepared two of the bedrooms and the other was used as storage. Looking at the small bed that Mason slept in each night, she knew it wasn't big enough for two people. Roberta entered the room behind Abby and asked, "Whose room is this?"

Abby hesitated but decided that the truth was the only answer. "Mason sleeps in here, but I'm sure he'll sleep in the bunkhouse until we can prepare the other bedroom. I'll sleep in here and you and Uncle Jackson can have my room."

***

After the sleeping arrangements were made and the rooms were prepared, Roberta announced that she was going to retire for the evening. They had traveled for several days and she was exhausted. Abby said that she was going to retire too.

Later that evening when everyone had settled down for the night, Mason knocked softly on Abby's bedroom door and entered. He took a seat on the side of Abby's bed. He was thrilled that her memory had returned and she seemed to be herself again. But he was still upset that she was doing too much and not resting.

"How are you feeling, sweetheart," he asked gently. He took her hand and kissed the center of her palm.

"My mind had been racing from one thought to another, and with all the extra work today because of the unexpected guests, I am just plain tuckered out. Tomorrow will be better. I was surprised to see Lucinda, but I am glad that she's leaving in the morning. She frightens me," she said as she covered a yawn with her other hand. "I am thrilled that your uncle and Roberta are here."

"Me too, I wish Uncle Jackson would settle here with us or nearby for sure. I'm going to ask him to do that. Would you like that, too?"

"Wonderful," she said, yawning again and trying to keep her eyes open.

"One more question before you go off to dreamland. What did you and Paul talk about?"

"Oh, just about how I feel and my memories," she said as she closed her eyes.

"Good night, sweet girl," he said as he leaned over and kissed her soft lips.

## Chapter 28

Early the next morning before the sun came up over the trees, Mason shook Buster awake. "Sorry, sir, I didn't mean to oversleep," he said as he rubbed the sleep out of his eyes.

"You didn't oversleep, but I need for you to get ready and follow Lucinda's covered wagon until you think they won't turn around and head back this way. I don't trust them." Mason paced as Buster threw on his clothes and boots. "I have prepared you a couple of ham biscuits to eat on the trail. Stay out of sight. I don't want them to know that they are being followed." The creeping of wagon wheels sounded behind the barn. He watched as the old woman with her driver turned the mules down the trail toward Eagle's Station. Buster headed into the barn to saddle his horse.

"Be careful, boy. See you tonight." Mason returned

to the kitchen where Abby was sitting at the table, sipping a fresh cup of coffee.

"So, they're gone," Abby said as Mason poured himself a cup of the hot brew.

"Yes, I know you were fond of Lucinda as a child, but I'm happy to say that she is out of our lives forever."

Abby's sadness showed on her sweet face. "Abby, sweet, I think you're still tired from yesterday. Please allow me to hire another lady from the village to come in and help with the cooking. I believe another lady along with Cactus Flower can handle breakfast and the evening meal. It won't be long before Paul and his crew will be moving on to another part of the country. They've almost completed the clearing of my land so that will be seven fewer men to cook for."

"Oh, Mason, I really feel fine. It's just that I am remembering my mama and other things in my past. With the return of my memory, I feel I am reliving my mama's sickness and her death all over again. My heart is broken. I loved her so much." Tears fell down her soft white cheeks as Mason brushed them away with his finger.

His own eyes misted as he remembered a stranger coming to his friend's house and telling him that his own parents had died in a boating accident. Even though he was five and twenty now, he felt like he was nine all over again. Over the years he had been thankful for Uncle Jackson. And his uncle had taken on the role as guardian for Abby, after her mama died because she had no other family or real friends. Mason's life had changed since his uncle had sent Abby to him and he felt blessed to have her in his life.

***

Roberta was an early riser. She had dressed and prepared her hair for the day. Hurrying into the kitchen, she was surprised to see Mason and Abby already up and enjoying their coffee.

"Good morning," she said cheerfully. "I had planned to be up and get the biscuits started and slice the ham for breakfast. I enjoy cooking, and Abby, I was looking forward to letting you sleep in this morning."

Abby wiped her eyes and cleared her throat. "I appreciate the help. Cactus Flower will be here soon. If you start the biscuits, I will prepare the lumberjacks' lunch pails."

Cactus Flower helped Roberta make quick work of a hearty breakfast and helped with the lunches for the lumberjacks. Billy cooked breakfast in the bunkhouse for the ranch hands.

***

Uncle Jackson had risen early and went outside to watch for Paul Miller. He wanted to talk with him alone about Abby.

"Paul," Jackson said, "I remember you from San Francisco and I am sure you know who I am."

"Yes, I do remember you well. I have a lot to take care of this morning, but I would like to talk with you after breakfast tomorrow. I have a great deal to think about," Paul replied.

***

Dawn had deepened over the land and the sky blazed with melon-colored clouds. Abby loved this country. Just being able to walk outside and enjoy the fresh air and beautiful skies made her happy. She had more freedom here than she ever had in the big city.

Abby strolled out to the hen house and collected the eggs. She washed them on the back porch and placed them in a big pot, then covered the eggs with water and boiled them to go into the lunch pails for the men. After making several pies, she went and lay down for a short nap. Cactus Flower had made a pot of fresh vegetable soup and baked cornbread for the ranch hands' lunch. Tonight she was going to fry several chickens and have some leftover soup for supper, so Abby enjoyed a few moments' rest.

The house was quiet now that everyone was busy working or visiting. Since Abby had been a little under the weather, The Old Wise Woman didn't let the children come and visit with her. She missed them. Tomorrow, she thought, I will send a message and invite them to come and see me.

***

Roberta and Uncle Jackson had returned from the

trading post. Mrs. Peterson insisted that they stay for the noon meal. Roberta had purchased a bag full of items, even though Jackson had told her over and over that he had sent the things to the store and she didn't have to pay for them. But pay she did.

"I got a few things that we needed and the poor man has a family and children to support. I couldn't just take the things without paying for them," she declared. Jackson gave up trying to make her understand about the business deal he had with Mr. Peterson.

"Supper smells wonderful, Cactus Flower," Roberta said as she placed a big white apron over her dress. "After supper, I'll wash the dishes while you rest."

***

When all the men had completed the evening meal and gone off to the bunkhouse or their tents in the woods, Mason and Jackson went into the parlor to discuss the idea of building a house on the north side of Mason's property. Jackson had not yet spoken with Roberta about living here at Eagle's Nest.

## Chapter 29

Early the next morning, Roberta, Abby and Cactus Flower were in the kitchen cooking breakfast for the lumberjacks and placing sandwiches and sweet rolls in their lunch pails. Hot coffee was brewing on the stove as everyone filed into the kitchen for the morning meal.

Abby hurried down into the cellar to get some wild strawberry jam when she overheard Paul and Jackson having a conversation. "You know that I am aware that you're Abby's father," Uncle Jackson said.

Abby stopped on the ladder, listening as their voices faded away. But the words that she had heard penetrated her mind over and over. *Paul was her father.* She was trying to absorb what Uncle Jackson had said. Paul Miller, the lumberjack and doctor, was her papa, the man that she only knew as a new friend.

With the closing of the screen door, the sound snapped her back to reality. She continued up the ladder and placed the two jars of jam on the ground. There was no way she could face anyone until she got her mind wrapped around the idea that Paul was her papa.

She ambled away from the ranch house and recalled the funny feeling that she had when meeting Paul for the first time. It was as if she knew him and now she connected the feelings.

Abby strolled on the path to the trading post. As she walked tears flowed down her stark white face and her knees felt like they might give away. Stepping off the trail into the woods she discovered a fallen log. Abby sat down, placed her face in her hands and silently cried.

"Abb-y, who has hurt you?" Running Bear said as he raced over to her.

Glancing up, Abby saw the two children she had grown to love. Little Beauty stood close to her side, holding a basket with a few pecans.

"Oh, Running Bear," Abby said, as she took the bottom of her dress and wiped her eyes. "No one has hurt me—."

"Why you cry like a papoose?"

"Come and sit in my lap, you two. Little Beauty, I have missed both of you so much."

"Old Wise Woman wouldn't let us come because you were sick. You better now?" Little Beauty asked as she rubbed a tear off Abby's cheek.

"Yes, I'm better, now that you two are with me."

"I miss your pies," the little girl said, smiling.

"Abby! Abby," a voice called her name from a distance. Abby and the two children sat frozen, not answering the call.

In a few minutes, Mason appeared with his hands on his hips and his boots spread wide apart. His expression changed from relief to anger.

"What are you doing out here away from the house by yourself? We have a search party out looking for you, and here you sit. I have a good mind to turn you over my knee and paddle your backside."

Running Bear quickly slid from Abby's lap and pulled out his small sharp knife from the scabbard that he wore on his hip. He took a warrior's stance and waved the blade back and forth in front of Mason.

"You'll have to kill me first. You'll not harm my woman!"

Mason was so taken back that he didn't know how to respond to the six-year-old fierce warrior, Abby's protector.

Abby stood, smiling at Mason. She asked Running Bear for the knife. He reluctantly handed it to her. She placed the knife back in his scabbard and gave him a hug.

"Now, let's go have some breakfast."

Running Bear looked up at Mason and back to Abby. "What about him?" Running Bear asked as he pointed at Mason.

"Oh, him," she said with a grin. "He wouldn't harm a fly much less me."

After returning to the house, Roberta and Jackson were very pleased to meet the two Indian children. Beauty immediately took to Roberta while Running Bear trailed after the older White man, Uncle Jackson.

Paul knocked on the back door after lunch. "Abby, would you come and have a talk with me, please?"

"Certainly," she replied as she wiped her hands and removed her white apron. She took his hand and they strolled to the front of the house. He motioned to the porch swing and they sat for a few minutes gazing out over the front yard.

"Abby, may I see the locket that you wear around your neck?"

Abby pulled the necklace over her head and watched Paul unsnap the locket. "You know, I remember the day Bella and I had these pictures made so many years ago."

"I never saw my mama without this locket around her neck. She never took it off until she was dying and she placed it on mine."

"You have to know that you're the spitting image of her with your sparkling green eyes and lovely blonde hair. She was the most beautiful woman in all of San Francisco."

"If you felt that way, why did you leave us and never return? My mama worked hard to support us."

"I'm sorry, but tell me about your childhood," Paul

said.

Sitting quietly for a few minutes, Abby continued. "I had dinner with mama every night. Afterward, she would dress in colorful satin gowns and place pretty peacock feathers in her golden hair. She painted her face and wore bright red paint on her lips. With her beautiful face, I often wondered why she would want to cover it with that face paint." She watched Paul's reaction as she talked about her mama. He made no comment.

"At school, the girls and boys would not play with me. I wasn't picked to play in any of the schoolyard games or invited to any of their birthday parties. One day, a mean girl made nasty remarks to me about my mama and what she did in the saloon. Other children called me ugly names until a new teacher threatened to punish them if they didn't leave me alone. I guess the teacher took pity on me, because she gave me books to read at recess and allowed me to take them home. Once we went to a church service and we sat on the back pew. Everyone who was sitting near us got up and moved as far away as they could. We never went back."

Paul's eyes were misty, but he still didn't make a remark about anything she was telling him.

"I had no friends. I felt like a prisoner in the only home I ever knew, the saloon." Tears slid from her eyes, but she wiped them away with the back of her hand. "There were many rooms off limits to me and I could only go outside if Mama or Lucinda were with me. Mama became very ill and I nursed her the best I knew how. But, before Mama died, she instructed me to go see Mr. Jackson Waters, Mason's uncle. I had never heard his name before or even seen him. But when he took me away from the saloon and offered to send me here to marry his nephew, I readily agreed. He offered me freedom and a real home."

Abby gazed out over the lovely yard that soon would be covered with white snow. Paul cleared his throat. "Abby, I am sorry that you had a bad time growing up because of where your mama worked. Things would have been different if I hadn't run off and left both of you. The only excuse I have is that when I returned to town and found your mama working in that…place, I went a little crazy and never gave her a chance to explain. I ran away and left both of you behind. I tried hard to bury my past, changed my name, but I did think of you often. I am sorry. I would like to continue to be your friend, if you can forgive me."

"Are you saying that you don't want to be my papa?"

"Heavens no! I want that more than anything, but I didn't know if you could ever forgive me enough and that you might only allow me to be your friend."

"I was small when you went away, but I felt something special about you the first time I met you. I think in my heart I knew who you were from the first. Yes, I want you to be my papa."

***

The days were filled with cooking for everyone—cleaning, washing and sewing new draperies for the parlor. Each night for a week, Abby and Paul embraced each other's company. They sat in the parlor as Paul told of his life after leaving San Francisco, chapter by chapter. He touched Abby's heart as he explained his decision to give up being a doctor. After weeks of being trapped in the mining cave with two other men who were severely hurt, he couldn't save them. With only a limited amount of medical supplies, no food and little water, the men died. He vowed that he never wanted to witness people dying while he cared for them.

Abby shook her head as a mist gathered behind her beautiful eyelids, letting Paul know that she understood.

"While traveling," he continued, "I stopped at a lumberjack camp and hired on as a tree-trimmer. Later, I decided to become a lumberjack and I worked myself up to become the best lumberjack in the business." Paul sat quietly for a minute remembering the long hard hours he put in each day.

"I got to travel all over the northern states, and I have met so many wonderful people. I did work for Mr. Peterson, and soon I met Mason, one of the finest young men I've ever been around," Paul said.

One night as she and her newly discovered Papa talked, he wanted to know even more about her. Abby had already told him about her childhood, but he wanted to know everything about her—her schooling and other activities. She took several deep breaths, opened her heart and unveiled her lonely and sad childhood. First, she expressed how she had prayed for his return—a man whom she faintly remembered, but the man whom her mama had longed for.

Paul was saddened that he had caused his only child to have such an awful childhood. Abby did assure him that she was loved and cared for by her mama and the people who lived in the saloon.

One night, Paul came into the parlor and told Abby that he had spent most of the day helping to deliver an Indian baby. "The Old Wise Woman sent for me and asked if I would help her with the delivery. After hours of labor, the baby wouldn't come on its own. After examining the mother, I discovered the baby was turned wrong. I could feel the infant's feet. With the mama's help, I was able to turn the baby and within minutes, a big healthy boy slid out into the Old Wise Woman's hands—a new life, another one of God's greatest miracles."

***

Abby clapped and laughed until Mason couldn't listen to the fun they were enjoying without him. He entered the parlor and saw his wife wrapped in the arms of her papa.

"Come in, Mason, and sit down with us. I've decided to sell my lumberjack business and reopen my doctor's practice," he said as he pulled Abby close.

"That's wonderful," Mason said, as he watched the joy on his wife's face. "Where are you going to practice?"

"I wanted to discuss this with you and Abby before I made a final decision. Mr. Peterson has agreed to sell me a piece of his land at Eagle's Station. I'd like to build an infirmary with an apartment connected to the back for my living quarters."

"Paul, I think that would be wonderful. You'll be close by, and Eagle's Station and the surrounding areas could use a good doctor." Mason walked over and shook Paul's hand and patted him on the back.

"What do you think, Abby?" Mason asked.

"I am thrilled. Our children will have a grandfather close by."

Mason's heart leaped. This was the first hint that Abby was going to be a real wife to him.

"I have some news to report to both of you," Mason said. "Uncle Jackson and Roberta want to build a house nearby. After taking care of his business in San Francisco, they will settle here with us." He glanced at Abby who eyes sparkled with fresh tears.

"Abby, aren't you happy about the news? First, your papa will be living a few miles from here and now Uncle Jackson and Roberta will be close, too."

"Oh, Mason, my heart runneth over with happiness. I already have new friends and now to have a house filled with family makes me the happiest girl alive."

## Chapter 30

Late that evening, Mason's heart was filled with joy. Abby had given him a sign that she wanted to be his wife in more than name only. After Paul left the parlor to return to his sleeping quarters in the bunkhouse, Mason headed to the kitchen while Abby went to her room. Tonight would be the night that he had been putting off for weeks. It was time to ask Abby about how she came to be at his ranch.

As Mason entered Abby's room, she was standing near the small bed. When she looked up at him, she said, "You know, Mason, we've got to get a bigger bed in here. As my husband, you cannot stay out in the bunkhouse forever. The men will begin to talk." Mason nearly yelled from relief. He was thrilled that Abby was talking about their relationship. It was time to make her his wife.

"They're already talking," he said, sheepishly. "But, Abby, you and I need to have a very crucial conversation. After everyone has settled in for the night, let's meet in the parlor and have a talk."

Roberta and Uncle Jackson seem to linger a long time in the kitchen. Finally, they said their good nights and headed to bed. The other guest room that had been used for storage had finally been made up for them.

Mason went into the parlor and opened his Bible. He stared at the pages but couldn't seem to focus on any of the words. Closing the book, he prayed that God would give him the correct words to use as he questioned Abby about her past.

Abby knocked on the parlor door before she entered. Mason had been praying. Abby lingered by the door. "Oh, excuse me."

"You're fine. Come and take a seat in this rocker," he said as he pulled it closer to the fireplace and placed the Bible back on the mantle. "Come and sit down next to me. I enjoy sitting in a rocker. I know you do, too."

"Yes, my mama had one placed in my room, and I would rock my dolls to sleep," she said, smiling at the memory. She smoothed her skirt over her lap and relaxed, then gave an unladylike yawn before she could help herself. "I'm sorry. I guess I'm tired too." She laughed at herself.

This is nice, Mason thought, as he sat beside Abby in front of the fireplace in his new parlor. This was just like he had planned. He needed to know all about this girl, who had been his wife in name only for several months. He had already completely lost his heart to her.

"I asked Uncle Jackson about your past, but he said that I should ask you and only you. So would you like to begin?" Before she could answer, he suggested that she start at the first time she met his uncle Jackson.

"I think I should start at the very beginning, so you'll understand where I came from and why and how I met your uncle." She gave Mason a candid look without blinking an eye.

*Oh, Lord, please give me the grace to accept this girl. Let me forgive her for all of her past sins, for I know that I am not to judge her,* he prayed silently as he prepared for the worst.

"My mama was sick for several weeks. She had been sick off and on many times the last year, but this time she knew she wasn't going to get well. My mama was Isabella Mills, the head madam at The Red Dog Saloon. You lived in San Francisco for many years, so I know you have heard about and seen the place."

She waited until Mason said yes that he remembered the saloon.

"It was a busy saloon before the gold strike, and later it burned down in the biggest fire San Francisco ever had, but it was soon rebuilt. We didn't live there until the new one was completed. My mama took in washing and ironing, but when the fire burned over half of the town, people left the city and mama lost her customers. So one day, we packed our meager belongings and entered the back door of the saloon, and that became my home until I came here."

"How old were you then?" Mason asked.

"Three or four. The schoolhouse didn't burn, so when I was old enough I went to school. Lucinda or Mama would walk me to and from the school every day. I had no friends because the kids weren't allowed to play with me. My mama worked in a bad place, a little girl told me one day."

"The saloon's cook wasn't friendly, but Lucinda made her teach me to cook. I loved making pies. I learned to wash, iron, sew and clean. After school, I had chores to do, but I got to eat dinner each evening with Mama. That was really the only time I got to be with her. Lucinda was like a mother to me, but I never felt that she loved me." Abby paused and took a breath.

"After mama took ill the last day before she died, she told me to go see your uncle. She made me promise that I would move out of the saloon and get away from San Francisco. She said your uncle would help me and for me to listen to him."

Abby pulled her hanky out of the sleeve of her dress and wiped her eyes. "I had never met your uncle or even heard his name before." She sat very still, not moving or rocking.

"So you went to see my uncle, and what did he do for you?"

"Oh, sorry, I forgot what I was saying. I miss my mama so much." She wiped her eyes again and said,

"He helped me. He wouldn't allow me to go back to the saloon, and I went to his lovely home and met Roberta. She took me under her wing, just like a mama hen. I had to bury Mama, but your uncle went to the funeral with me. I was so surprised at how many people attended the service. Some of the men took up a collection of money for me. So sweet. I didn't need their money, but your uncle said I had to take it. He said they were taking care of Bella's child."

Anyway, later your uncle Jackson read your letter to me, asking for a bride. Well, when your uncle gets an idea or plan, you'd better get out of his way," she laughed.

"Since you needed or wanted a bride and I needed to get away from San Francisco, a perfect plan was formed by your uncle. So, here I am, your bride, and I am away from that terrible city."

"Yes, I can see how you came to be here. How long did you live at Uncle Jackson's home?"

"I was there for nearly a month because he had to choose the equipment and furniture that you had requested. It took time for him to select just the right men to work for you, too."

They sat back in their rockers and stared into the fire without speaking. Mason wasn't completely satisfied with her answers about living in the saloon. She said she learned to cook, sew, clean and wash and iron, but what about her other duties? He had to ask. *Lord, help me*, Mason prayed silently. He had to know if he was married to a decent girl or a soiled dove. Giving himself a little shake, he found the courage to finally ask her.

"Abby, I have to ask a question that you didn't answer for me. Please understand—I need to know," he said as he studied her eyes.

Abby stopped rocking and sat still. Her face paled. He hadn't intended to scare her, but it seemed he had. Finally, he took a deep breath as Abby stared down at her lap.

*Will she tell the truth to this critical question*? I have prayed to accept her answer, however bad it is. *Lord, please help me*, he prayed again.

Mason leaned forward in his rocker. "Abby, when you lived upstairs in The Red Dog Saloon, did you give pleasure to strange men for gold nuggets or paper money?"

There! He had asked, and she had not jumped up and rushed out of the room. She shut her eyes and seemed to be studying her reply.

Abby sat as still as a stone statue. She took in a big breathe and sighed. "Before I answer your question, I have to know something. You have declared your love for me and in return I have grown to love you more than words could ever describe. I truly need an honest answer from you." Pausing, she glanced around the cozy room. Mason's Bible was placed on the fireplace mantle.

"You seem to be obsessed with wanting to know about my past. So, I need to know if I had given pleasure to, as you so gently phrased it, to strange men, would it make a difference to you.

Abby's insides were twisted into knots and she felt that she might lose her supper at any minute. But, before she could move, Mason had slipped to the floor on his knees and clutched both of her hands.

"Abby, my love. I had no right, no right at all to ask you that ugly question. Please forgive me. I love you with all my heart and soul and nothing in your past could change the way I feel for you. If my words have hurt you, I am so sorry. I have prayed whether I should ask you or not, but I have struggled from the hearsay that I heard and I wanted to tear those men from limb to limb. The thoughts of some unworthy man touching you made me sick. I have prayed to God to give me the wisdom to not bring up the subject of other men, but I am a stupid fool. Please, forgive me, for I know there's nothing that would cause me to love you less." Taking both of her hands, he kissed them and attempted to pull Abby into his arms.

"Mason, please. I have never been with a man, strange or otherwise. Does that answer your doubts about me?"

"Yes, love, but in my heart I can honestly say that it wouldn't have matter."

"You don't know how much that statement pleases me." Abby reached and laid her palm on his face.

"That's what I want to do every day; please you."

"Mason," Abby whispered as she placed two fingers

over his lips to keep him quiet, "your uncle would have helped me get away from that awful city, no matter what he thought of me, but he would have never chosen me to be your bride if I had been a soiled dove. He loves you so much."

"I know he does and I love him. He's been like a father to me," he said with a lump in his throat.

"But Mason, in the letter he wrote to you about me—the one you never received—you  must know that he did ask that we have time to become better acquainted before we consummated our marriage."

"I believe you. That sounds like something he would do. My uncle used to be a rough-neck, but a gentleman at heart when it came to the ladies." Mason smiled and pulled Abby out of the rocker into his arms.

"I love you, Abby. I have loved you for so long," he whispered into her golden hair.

"I have loved you too, but I've been so afraid, afraid that I wouldn't know how to give my love to you."

Abby felt as if her body had awakened with love such as she had never known could exist.  She had never been happier.

Pleased with each other's declaration of love, they walked hand in hand down the hall to their bedroom. Before entering the room, she stopped and gazed up at Mason. "I want to be your wife in every way."

"Yes," he said softly, and pulled her closer and kissed her. He felt her lips quiver beneath his. He knew that she was his and only his.

Other Books by
Linda Sealy Knowles

Journey to Heaven Knows Where
Hannah's Way
The Secret
Bud's Journey Home
Always Jess
Kathleen of Sweetwater, Texas

Coming soon:
Joy's Cowboy

Linda Sealy Knowles is an historical-romance-western writer that brings her love stories and characters to life. She gives God the glory for her talent that has given her much joy and happiness. Since 2012, she has written six novels. Linda is from Satsuma, Alabama but resides in Niceville, Florida, near her daughter, Kelli, and son, Pete, II. She has three lovely teenage granddaughters.

www.ingramcontent.com/pod-product-compliance
Lightning Source LLC
Chambersburg PA
CBHW072257130726
47910CB00012B/2067